DARK DECEPTION

THE DARK CREATURES SAGA - BOOK 3

ELLA STONE

ALSO BY ELLA STONE

Dark Creatures Prequel Novellas

Mother of Wolves

Son of a Vampire

Man and Wolf

Call of the Grimoire

The Dark Creatures Saga

Dark Creatures

Dark Destiny

Dark Deception

Dark Redemption

Dark Reckoning

The Bloodsuckers Blog Series

Life Sucks

Love Bites

Lost Souls

This story is a work of fiction. All names, characters, organisations, places, events and incidents are products of the author's imagination or are used fictitiously. Any resemblance to any persons, alive or dead, events or locals is entirely coincidental.

Text copyright © 2021 Ella Stone

Second edition published 2024

Paper Cat Publishing

ISBN: 979-8751221799

Edited by Carol Worwood

All rights reserved.

No part of this book should be reproduced in any way without the express permission of the author.

1

Narissa

I can't help but think of my dad as I sit here looking at an empty diary. I found it in the house we squatted in before this one. It's not leather like his were but covered in a cream fabric that's gone brown in patches and threadbare in others. I picked up a handful of pens there as well and shoved them in my pocket, although I've not actually written anything yet. We've now spent two weeks hiding in this run-down wooden-framed cottage in the middle of nowhere. Most of the time, I've been staring at the blank pages wondering what I should write. The thing is, so much has happened, where would I even start?

It's been three months since I discovered I'm a werewolf and almost all of that time has been spent on the run, travelling through Europe: across northern France, on to Germany, then settling near Munich for a while. Most of this has been undertaken on foot, walking, trekking, only now and then hitch-hiking or slipping onto crowded trains where we can get away without paying. Money is tight. No credit cards. No ATM withdrawals. Nothing that can be used to trace our movements.

This latest hideout is a crumbling shack in the Austrian mountains near the town of Innsbruck, and every day we spend here feels like a week. All I want to do is run back home, but I don't even know where home is. It's certainly not my mother's werewolf pack. I made sure of that with the stupid, impulsive behaviour that led to me being cast out as a lone wolf, away from its protection. And London? Well, there's nothing there for me now, either. The thing is, while I don't know where I belong, it sure as hell is not here, doing nothing just like yesterday and the day before and the day before that. Just waiting for something to happen. For anything to happen.

I'm still gazing vacantly into space when what's left of the door creaks open and Oliver steps inside. He left before I woke up this morning, which is generally what happens. It's impossible to understand how two people can spend so much time together and say so little. Some days, he can barely look at me, let alone speak to me, and every conversation we have ends up with the two of us bickering, like an old couple whose marriage has run its course. Not that we've ever been in that kind of relationship and I sure as hell don't know what you'd call what we have now.

What's so crap is that I can't blame him for acting this way with me. It's fair to say I brought this on myself. Thanks to my mistakes, our Rey is dead and Oliver got beaten to a pulp before having to abandon his life and the job he loved to go on the run with me. I guess it's easy to see why I'm not his favourite person at the moment. To make matters worse, he'd barely started recovering from his injuries before he had to sweep in with a helicopter to fly me away from the pack. And with all this walking, nights spent sleeping on hard floors and days searching for food, I'm not sure he's ever going to heal properly. Not that I'd admit that to his face.

He's holding a pair of brown birds, their dead heads dangling. I guess this is our dinner tonight.

"Have you been anywhere today?" he asks, dropping them on the dilapidated kitchen table and starting to pull out handfuls of feathers.

I feel myself bristling.

"Is there somewhere you needed me to go?"

"No. I just thought you might take a run. It's important to keep up changing into a wolf. You must make sure you can do it immediately, if you have to."

"It's not something I'm likely to forget."

"Maybe so, but don't you also need to do it to stop feeling caged in or whatever it is?"

I snort in response. I don't mean to sound like a bitch but really.

"You think changing into a wolf is going to make me feel less trapped, less helpless than the fact I don't know what's going on with my family? Did you hear from Calin today? It's been a month now. You said you were going to find a way to contact him."

"No, I didn't. I said *he'd* find a way to contact *us* and then only if he has to. You know that, Narissa. Otherwise we'll all be at risk."

"What about Blackwatch? You could see if someone there could get hold of him."

"I told you what Calin said to me before we left. I have to keep Blackwatch out of this, until he has a better idea of what's going on."

"But it's been a month," I repeat. "Surely, he should know more by now. Besides, Blackwatch are the ones who keep the peace. There shouldn't be any danger there."

"I don't know, Naz. I really don't. Perhaps having a member of their organisation helping the vampires' most wanted fugitive, isn't good for vampire-human relations. I'm just following orders and keeping you hidden."

This isn't the first time we've had this conversation. If I was smart, I'd give it up now, but I've been distinctly lacking in common sense recently.

"He can't have meant for us to stay like this for so long. I don't understand why he didn't give you more to go on. He trusted you enough to lend you his helicopter."

"He paid for a helicopter which I left where he told me. Do you think I'm hiding things from you? I'm not the one who lies and keeps secrets around here, remember?"

Well, it didn't take long for him to throw that back in my

face again. There are a dozen responses I can think of. A dozen snide retorts or quick-witted jibes to bite back with. But the fact is, it's true. None of this is his fault and me behaving like a bitch isn't helping one bit. Sucking in a deep breath, I stand up and move over to the table and peer at the dead birds.

"Here, I can help with that."

"It's fine, I've got it."

As he plucks out another handful of feathers, he winces and grabs his shoulder.

"You need to rest," I say, sliding the second bird over towards me. "You haven't recovered yet."

"I'm not going to heal if I don't eat, am I?"

Food. Prior to this, my diet had comprised of almost solely fast food. Now we eat whatever we can lay our hands on. Safe to say, I'm getting pretty sick of it.

"It's not working, Oliver, staying out here in the middle of nowhere. You know it isn't. No wonder Calin hasn't contacted us. We should head to a city. It'd be easier for him to locate us there. And we could get jobs too, earn some money while we wait for him to find us, rather than living hand-to-mouth like this."

"Or you could just change and catch us some food, so I don't have to do everything?"

"I told you, that's not an option."

This is another massive bone of contention. I know things would be easier if I went out for a few hours and caught us, say, a few rabbits. I'm pretty sure I could do it easily enough, although I've never hunted anything in my life before. But that's not the issue and I really do feel bad that I haven't. The problem is the silence.

I have changed periodically since I left the pack, but only when the caged wolf in me needed a release and never for more than a few minutes at a time. Certainly not long enough to catch the scent of something we could eat, chase it down and kill it. No, it's the emptiness that's overwhelming.

I decided to become a lone wolf before I left the pack, without realising the consequences. I seem to specialise in making hasty, badly considered choices. But back then, the silence seemed so much better than having people constantly invading my mind without my say-so. But this is different. There's no one here to let in or keep out. Nothing. Just me and my thoughts, and that's something I can't deal with now. Just a few seconds at a time is all I can take.

"There's a lake a few miles from here," Oliver says, continuing to pluck. "I saw it from the hillside. I'll go tomorrow. See if I can catch us some fish."

"Great. It's been over a week since I last had to deal with fish guts."

I meant the comment in jest, but from the way he turns around scowling, he doesn't see the funny side.

"What do you expect of me, Naz? What is it you want? I didn't have any time to plan for this, but I'm doing my best, okay? I'm sorry the food isn't up to the culinary standards you and your vampire were obviously enjoying with the pack, but I honestly don't know what more I can do here right now."

Silence follows. I can see that this would be a good time to say I'm sorry. I should thank him for everything he's done and apologise for spending ninety-nine percent of the time since he rescued me being a complete and utter bitch. But what I should do and what I'm able achieve, seem to be at odds lately.

"I just want to get away from here," I protest. "That's all. It's been months, Oliver. Months of us bickering in one filthy, damp place after another. I'm going insane. The solitude is driving me crazy. I need to see other people. Can't we just head to a city somewhere? Hide out amongst other humans?"

"Every city has vampires and that means the Vampire Council could hear about us."

"I get that. I do, and I know the Council is after me, but honestly, how would anyone over here recognise me? We're hundreds of miles away from London, from anyone who has the vaguest idea what I look like."

"It's too big a risk."

"No, staying like this is a risk. How do you think this is going to work long term, Oliver? I can't stay like this. I really can't. It's not caged wolf you have to worry about here. It's caged human."

"And where do you think we should go, exactly?"

"I don't care. Just as long as there are other people. I can't cope with the emptiness of this, Oliver."

He shakes his head, but I'm sure his resolve is weakening. At least I hope it is, and I'm not done yet.

"You said yourself, if there were anything major we

should know about, Calin would've let us know somehow. We need to earn money so we can get some proper food. You do see that, surely?"

He has now finished plucking his bird, while mine still rests intact in my hand, the last of its warmth slowly seeping away. I want to press him, to say more, but I don't. I wait. Finally, as he reaches across and takes the carcass from me, he grunts.

"Fine then. We'll head to a city. But on one condition. Let me teach you how to fight."

"I can fight."

"As a human."

"I'm a pacifist now. No more fighting. Not on my watch, ever."

"Then I guess we're staying put."

2

Calin

I used to love the taste of a good-quality whisky. A rich, amber, velvety syrup, the type I'd would never have been able to afford when I was human. In fact, I'm not sure I'd ever even tried it then, certainly not an expensive one. Cheap ale and moonshine were about the best I could run to. Not that I remember those flavours now.

When I was changed, so many of my senses were altered too, generally for the better. Hearing, sight, my sense of smell, all of them improved, heightened in ways I'd never have imagined possible. To be able to detect the heartbeat of a hummingbird or catch the scent of fresh bread from five streets away, these are gifts. Small reminders of the great legacy bestowed on me. But taste is the one where it all gets a little complicated. I can distinguish between the different blood types, for example. That sense is heightened, but it's very specific. Blood alone is the one thing that contains all those human umami flavours: bitterness, sweetness, dense meaty richness. A thousand nuances in a single droplet. But the old-fashioned taste buds are gone. I can chew and swallow, perpetuate the illusion of normality if I must, but there is no pleasure in it. And yet whisky—so long as it's the best of the best—still offers that gentle burn when I swallow it. That illusive and unique sensation which is almost, but not quite, human.

Unfortunately, no amount of expensive alcohol can counteract the taste of the bile that rises in my throat, like a slow acting poison, every time my mind goes back to what happened in the forest.

Narissa had joined me in the clearing where I'd arranged for Oliver to meet us by helicopter, when the gunshot rang out. That single round, which sent the birds flying from their perches and animals racing for cover. Then came the howling. I will not profess to know anything about the way of wolves, after only spending such a short time amongst them, but I knew it could only have meant one thing. And as Narissa wrapped her arms around me, I couldn't bring myself to tell her. If I had, she wouldn't have left. She would have raced back to the village and got herself killed, or worse.

Yet here I am, months later. What's my excuse now? What's the reason that I still haven't told her what happened, even though she's miles away from that danger?

CHAPTER 2

The truth is, I can't bring myself to risk speaking to her, so fearful am I of what I might say. I don't want to lie to her, not after everything we've been through, and I can't bear to be the one to break it to her.

When the helicopter left, all hell broke loose. Some wolves fled to the forest. Some went for the vampires. Me? I kept out of sight. A hundred-and-twenty-plus years of life, and when the wolfpack needed me—when Narissa's family needed me—I hid. Maybe that's the reason I've been getting through so much whisky lately. To try and blur the memory, the way it would have worked for the old me. Unfortunately, like so many other moments in my past, I know there's nothing that will shut those thoughts out.

It's harder at times like this, when I'm on my own. I keep telling myself it was the right thing to do. And it's true. I know it was. I could have fought with the wolves. I could have helped them, but staying hidden was the only option if I was to stand a chance of clearing Narissa's name. If any vampires had seen me there with the wolves, they would have made the link between us.

The vampires didn't search the forest for long. The risk of getting torn apart by furious werewolves must have outweighed their desire to find her. So, I bided my time in the shadows, waiting for them to leave.

When the coast was clear and it was safe to return to the village, the sun had set, and the place was like a ghost town. The air was still. Even the birds were silent. It reminded me of the war, after a battle, when the shelling had stopped and the cries of the injured had ceased, for the worst possible reason, a hush falling on the fields as if all forms of life had deserted them.

Standing by the well, I waited until she came. Praying she would.

"Calin."

Chrissie walked towards me, blood stained and exhausted. Yet her eyes still had a glimmer of hope in them. At least that was one way I hadn't let her down.

"Please tell me she got away."

"She got away."

"Thank God."

"Freya?"

Her head slumped forward—all the answer I needed.

"Of all the cowardly things to do. To not even offer her a fair fight. Never, in all the history of wolves …" I try to express something, but my words fail me.

"Why would they do that? Why would they shoot her?"

"Why on earth would Juliette side with the vampires? One thing is certain though, she planned this with them. Orchestrated the chaos Freya's murder has created. But none of it makes sense and I don't know what I'm supposed to do."

"You must take what's left of your pack somewhere you'll be safe."

Thinking back, this was such a stupid comment to make. Of course she was going to do that. Still, she smiled in that dignified way of hers.

"We've already split up. Some are heading deeper into the Highlands. Some, I fear, have followed Juliette. A few of us have stayed here to give Freya a proper funeral and say our farewell to her. It's the least she deserves."

"Do you need me to stay? Tell me how I can help you?"

With another smile that tore at my heart, she placed a hand on my shoulder.

"Keep Narissa safe. That is your only job now."

As I drove up the hillside away from the village, I noticed clouds of black rising from the canopy in my rear-view mirror. I slowed to a stop where it was possible to look out over the forest, and from there I watched as tendrils of smoke from Freya's funeral pyre drifted away and the sound of mournful howling echoed through the valley.

Although I should have headed straight to London before my absence was noted, I realised there was one more thing I could do.

When the smoke had ceased, I quickly ran back, and once certain the remaining pack members had left, I retrieved something from the cooling ashes—a single silver bullet.

3

Oliver

It's taken four hours to reach this lake, but thankfully, it's teaming with fish. So much so that I could probably reach in and grab one with my bare hands. Or at least I would once have been able to. No matter how I tried to deny it, Narissa was right last night when she said I haven't healed properly. My left arm and shoulder are still suffering the effects of the fight with Styx. It's even worse in the morning when the muscles have had time to stiffen overnight.

Despite everything, I gave in to her, but I still don't know if it was the right decision. When I left this morning, I promised that tonight would be the last we'd spend here before heading further east and finding a quiet town where we can stay. Maybe in Hungary or Slovakia, perhaps. Somewhere else far away from London and the vampires who are hunting her. Perhaps when we're around people, she'll let me train her to fight. It's something I've been wanting to do since the day I took her away from the pack, but like everything with Naz, it's an uphill battle. She doesn't want to change into the wolf; she doesn't want to learn to protect herself; she just wants to bury her head in the sand the whole damn time.

From my bag, I retrieve a folded tissue holding some of the leftover meat from last night's meal. I need to find somewhere shallow though, if I'm going to stand any chance of catching a fish without a proper rod.

My eyes scan along the water's edge and I've just spotted a place I think will do when a buzzing distracts me. It's so alien that it takes me a moment to recognise it. Digging down into the bottom of my bag, I pull out a phone that I've wrapped in a pair of my old boxers, where I knew there'd be no chance of Naz ever looking. It's the old type from over a decade ago, like a brick, that you could run over with your car and it would probably still survive. It's not mine; I left that in London in my haste to get away. This one was "borrowed" on the flight up to Scotland. I charge it in secret whenever we stay somewhere that's got electricity. There's only one person who would be calling me, someone I really don't feel in the mood to speak to. But I know I have no choice.

"Tell me you've got some news. Anything at all."

"How is she? How's she coping?"

This is always his first question, checking on her like I wouldn't tell him if something had happened. Then again, perhaps I wouldn't. I've worked with vampires for many years and I've never come across one I felt I could trust. Calin Sheridan is no exception. And the way he obsesses over her is not normal. The memory of them together in the forest just before I took her away in the helicopter—his arms holding her so tightly—makes me shudder.

"Is she transforming? You know she must."

God, this guy is a prick.

"She wants to speak to you," I finally get in. "She wants to know about her mother, that she's safe. What am I supposed to tell her? I can't even look her in the eye when she talks about Freya. Honestly, I hate this. I hate having to lie to her all the time. It's been months. When are you going to tell her the truth?"

There's a short pause on other end of the line before the vampire speaks again.

"This is not a good time."

"What a surprise. When exactly do you think it will be?"

"I understand your predicament. I don't want to lie to her either. But you said it yourself, she's not going to be able to handle this at the moment. Give me a few more weeks."

"A few more weeks! To do what, exactly? Have you made *any* progress with the Council? With Polidori?"

There's another pause, and I know the answer.

"Polidori has withdrawn in a manner I've never known

before. Additional security around him, meetings I'm not privy to with sub-committees."

"Well make yourself privy to them. You said there could be a war in the offing. Why don't you try Jessop then, go to Blackwatch?"

"Because ..."

"Because of what, Sheridan? I'm fed up with these conversations that lead nowhere. You expect me to blindly follow your instructions, to trust that you're looking out for Naz's best interests, when all you do is keep me in the dark. I want the truth, for crying out loud. What is it you're not telling me?"

"You just have to trust me," he says.

Seriously? This guy knows how to piss me off. Three months of this is enough. I'm done.

"No, actually I don't have to trust you. And the longer you carry on like this, hiding things from me, the less I think I should.

"So how about this? You come clean right now or Narissa gets her way, and it won't be any old city we'll be heading for tomorrow morning. It'll be straight back to London."

"You wouldn't."

"Why not? How the hell can you think she's safer with me and my busted body in the middle of bloody nowhere than she would be in London with Blackwatch to protect her."

"Because Blackwatch is the problem."

"What?" I shake my head, convinced I can't have heard

him properly. "Blackwatch is the problem? What's that supposed to mean?"

I hear him sucking on his teeth.

"I didn't tell you the truth about how Freya died," he says, eventually.

A breeze sweeps in across the lake, shaking the leaves in the trees.

"What do you mean? You said one of the vampires killed her."

"I know. I thought it was easier that way."

"Easier than what? What's the truth, Sheridan? How did Naz's mother die?"

He clears his throat before speaking.

"She was shot. Shot by a sniper from somewhere up in the hills—and it was a human. I smelled one as they approached, and when one didn't arrive with them at the village, I thought that I'd somehow got it wrong. Then, after Narissa left, I caught the scent again. They shot her dead before she'd even had the opportunity to stand up to Juliette. There was no fair fight. She didn't stand a chance."

"Oh God."

An ambush. The Alpha of South Pack and the vampires obviously never had any intention of negotiating. Deep down, I feel the slightest twinge of sympathy for Calin. At least I now know why he's avoided speaking to Naz. How the hell could he tell her something like that?

Bringing myself back to the moment, my mind returns to my original question.

"But that still doesn't explain why you won't go to

Jessop with this. According to Naz, he knew Freya. He could find this human."

"You don't get it, do you?"

"Get what."

"Freya was a werewolf. The Alpha of her pack. She was killed with a silver bullet, and by the smell of it, it had been dipped in aconite, too. It was designed with the sole intention of killing a wolf."

"So, it was planned. We know that."

"There's only one place that you could get hold of something like that."

My stomach starts to churn. The breeze gusts again, even stronger and colder. A few leaves fall, sending the fish darting away from the shallows. No wonder he didn't want to tell me the truth. But now he's on a roll.

"Tell me, Grey, who at Blackwatch has sole access to the armoury and how could someone shoot a bullet with such precision from nearly two miles out?"

Whether his question is rhetorical or not, it doesn't make any difference. I can't speak. We both know there's only one person who fits the bill, on both counts. There's only one man who could have managed that.

My fishing expedition is netting me missing information, if not food. I'm trying to make sense of what Sheridan is telling me, to come up with a reason why Jessop would want to kill Freya. Maybe he's got it wrong. Worse still, perhaps he's lying. But as much as it goes against the grain, I believe him. I can't stand the guy, but I don't think he's a liar, which makes his concern for Naz even more annoying. It's genuine. He honestly cares about her. I almost wish he didn't.

"We can't stay where we are," I tell him after a minute contemplating what I've just heard. "She's restless and she needs other people around her. Besides, she's agreed to let me teach her to fight, if I agree to us moving to a town."

I expected him to object, to offer me the usual spiel about keeping her hidden and protected. Instead, he says, "Lithuania," as if it needs no further explanation.

"Lithuania? Why?"

"The west coast was a stronghold for witches back before the Blood Pact. And even though they've gone, vampires still give the place a wide berth."

Lithuanian is far from my strongest language, but I know enough to get by.

"Lithuania it is, then."

He clears his throat again.

"I'll be in touch."

4

Narissa

I don't know what's up with Oliver, but something's definitely wrong. More wrong than usual, that is. When he came back, he was silent. Completely silent. Didn't ask me to help him gut the fish or light the fire to cook them. Didn't pester me about changing into the wolf or going for a run. Nothing. Nothing at all. If I didn't know better, I'd say he'd seen a ghost down by that lake. I'm at least eighty percent sure they don't exist, though. But the way things have been lately, I wouldn't rule anything out.

"We'll head further east," he says the next morning, when I wake up to find him with his rucksack packed and slung over his shoulder, that same faraway look in his eyes. "But we can't stop. There won't be many, if any, safe places to stay at night on the road, so we'll be better off just travelling through."

"Okay, I'm fine with that."

He nods. "Maybe you should change now. Go for a run or whatever. There won't be another chance for quite a while."

I considered saying no and insisting I'll be fine. But as I'm not sure that's entirely true, it's my turn to nod, and I head outside. There's a cloud of fog hanging over the mountain as I strip off my clothes and drape them over one of the rickety wooden window shutters. I'm only going to change for a short while, like always. One minute at most. No time for the silence to get me down.

The release the wolf feels at being allowed out is instant, yet so is the pain at the emptiness in my head. I wait, my four paws in the morning dew, the mist starting to form droplets on my coat. Listening. Wishing. Could there be wolves out there? Maybe they've been following us, trying to tell me it's safe to go back now. Perhaps, by staying human so much of the time, I've missed the opportunity of hearing from them.

Without thinking twice, I drop the blocks from my mind and throw my inner voice out as far as it will go.

Freya? Lou? Chrissie?

Nothing.

Mum? I try, instead.

Still nothing. The emptiness circles, pulling me down with each passing breath. I wait a moment longer—then give up.

CHAPTER 4

Shortbread. Black coffee.

A second later, it's my human feet that are cold and soaking wet as I grab my clothes and get dressed.

"Are you ready?" Oliver calls from the front of the building. "The sooner we get going, the better."

Hitchhiking always looks fun in the movies. Fraught with danger, obviously, but seriously cool. Road trips, with all the interesting characters they get to meet who tell them about their exciting, adventure-filled lives and leave your heart feeling just a little lighter. In the films, everyone wears tie-dye and lets their hair blow out of the open car window as they sit back with their eyes closed.

Turns out, life's not like that at all. The only people we've met are chain-smoking old men, with horrendous taste in music. Not to mention extremely poor personal hygiene. Some of the cars and vans that have stopped for us have contained enough rubbish to fill a small landfill. But beggars can't be chooser, as they say, and it's ending soon.

It's taken us four days solid to get to our destination. Apparently, we're heading north. We've had to travel on foot quite often to cross various borders. I'm not entirely sure where we are, but I don't want to expose my ignorance to Oliver by asking. I guess I'll find out when we get there.

What's really annoying about spending all this time

crammed into a back seat reeking of cigarettes, is that I know we could have got here faster. He would insist on switching cars at least every couple of hours, along with doubling back several times, on the off chance someone was following us. Considering how little traffic we saw on the roads, I think that was being overly cautious.

His continuing silence is wearing thinner by the day. It was one thing when we were walking, but inside a vehicle, in such close proximity, it makes the awkwardness between us even more obvious. And it's not like I haven't apologised. I don't know how many more times or different ways I can do that. I get it. I've been a screw-up since the first day he met me, when I was breaking into Blackwatch. But it's his refusal to look at me that's the worst. Like he can't even bring himself to make eye contact.

It's around nine in the evening when we reach the outskirts of a large town. In the distance, I can see massive cranes silhouetted against the setting sun. I can hear the clang of ships' bells and the mournful cry of gulls. I guess we must have arrived at a port.

We say goodbye to our current lift next to a graffitied bus stop. Half a dozen teenagers are smoking under the awning. I assume that this is just another of our pit stops. That we'll wait here for another car to pick us up and carry on again. This won't be the first grey town we've passed through.

I'll be honest, it's not the type of place I feel comfortable in, and the wolf has already begun growling in the back of my head. I'm not sure what it expects me to do. If anything goes wrong, turning into a wolf isn't going to help us keep a low profile. I know that's why Oliver wants to train me to fight. But the thing I've come to realise in the last few months, is that starting a fight is a darn site easier than stopping one. And they never end well.

One of the kids shouts something at us in a language I don't understand, and the others start laughing.

Oliver stops, turns and slowly walks towards them. Whatever he says, it shuts them up pronto, and a moment later, he's back at my side, walking on the footpath.

"What did they say?" I ask.

"Nothing of any interest," he replies.

"What did you say?"

"Nothing much."

"Great. About as thrilling as our conversations then," I mutter under my breath.

Talk about keeping me in the dark, although I shouldn't be surprised. This is the way it's been the entire time. It doesn't help that he's been able to speak to every person we've hitched a lift with, regardless of the country. I always promised myself I'd learn another language at some point. French, German, perhaps even Mandarin. But it's another of those things I've never got round to.

"We should be able to find somewhere to stay in the centre of town," he says, not bothering to slow his pace or even look at me as he speaks.

"We're staying here?"

I don't bother to hide the surprise in my voice.

"For now. Tomorrow I'll set about finding some work."

Wow. I quicken my pace until I'm back alongside him, this new information causing a sudden burst of energy.

"If we are staying here, I can work too. I can find a bar job or something."

"You need to stay out of sight."

"I can find work in a back-street bar."

"How about you just stay hidden?"

I have to literally bite my tongue to keep from saying something I'll regret. We're both tired, I remind myself. Really tired. I've managed some sleep—mainly to avoid the awkwardness with Oliver—but it's been barely more than catnaps. The constant change of vehicles, the poor-quality roads, not to mention the bad driving, were hardly conducive to restful slumber. I suspect he forced himself to stay awake the whole time. He must be shattered.

After another twenty minutes walking, we reach the town centre, which is actually far more picturesque than I would have imagined. A group of large white buildings criss-crossed with beams are intersected by a river that I assume leads to the docks. There's a selection of small shops lining a cobbled street and a few bars and restaurants with chairs and tables outside. It's not Paris. It's not London. But maybe it won't be the worst place in the world to stay.

We keep walking until Oliver comes to a stop outside one of the bars. I don't know why he's chosen this one, unless it's because it's the most derelict-looking place. The windows are coated with a thick layer of grime and the paint is peeling off the frames. The letters than once spelled out the name of the establishment are mostly missing. Two old men sit on stools, smoking cigarettes and scowling.

"You wait here," he says, acknowledging the men with a nod. "I won't be more than a couple of minutes. If anything happens, if anyone approaches you, yell. Don't do anything stupid. Get it?"

"By stupid you mean—"

"Anything. Don't do anything. Just stay here and don't move."

He disappears into the bar, leaving me with the two grumpy old men. Great.

Shifting my position, I look back down at the lights that are glinting off the river. It's a peaceful view, although the noise from the docks makes it a little less so. People. It's been a long time since we've been around any and I can feel that the wolf is nervous.

"It's okay," I whisper to myself. "We're going to be just fine."

While I understand that I'm not to move, it takes less than a minute before the old men's glowers grow so intense that it's making the wolf part really jittery. Like, any second, I'm going to turn and give them something to really worry about. Obviously, I know this is not going to happen. Still, for safety's sake, I move a few steps away to where there's an even better view of the river. A group of young women walk towards me giggling, their arms looped.

Oliver's sudden voice makes me nearly jump out of my skin.

"I thought I told you to stay outside the bar."

"I moved, like, three feet."

"Next time, stay where I tell you," he says, before marching straight past me and back the way we came.

"What are you doing? Where are you going," I ask, having sprinted to catch up with him.

"Where do you think I'm going? I've found us a place to stay."

5

Decor wise, chintzy doesn't even begin to cover it. Everything in the living room and two bedrooms is floral, including the curtains and the sofa. Even the carpet is a strange brown colour with large red and green blotches that I'm pretty sure at one time were flowers, too. There are net curtains at the windows and lace doilies on the coffee table and bedside cabinets. Pictures of flowers in floral vases are on all the walls except the ones with windows, of which there is one in the living room and another in the main bedroom. Both have views of the river. The other bedroom is little more than a boxroom, not that it matters. It feels like the Hilton compared to where we've been these past three months.

Gazing outside, I can't make out much more than the occasional glimmer of light on the river. While I'm admiring the view, Oliver is opening and closing every cupboard until he eventually finds what he's looking for and pulls out a pile of bedsheets—floral, of course—and pillows.

"You take the main bedroom. I'll sleep in the other one," he says, picking up his bag again. I guess that's my cue then.

"Goodnight," I say. "And I'm sorry for all this."

For a split second, his eyes hold mine, just like the old Oliver would have done, and his lips start to move as if he's about to say something. My heart stupidly flutters with hope. But in less than the blink of an eye, the moment has gone.

"Goodnight, Naz," is all he manages.

WHEN I WAKE UP THE NEXT MORNING, I FIND HIM ALREADY sitting at the dining room table, with what looks like the contents of his pockets spread out in front of him. The odd receipt has been crumpled and pushed to the side, and all that remains are just a couple of notes and a few dozen coins—mostly Euros and Sterling—but there seem to be a few other currencies in there too. Unfortunately, there's not a lot of any of them.

"This is what we're down to," he says, as I move into the kitchen to fill the kettle. "I paid up front for this place for a week, and it's low season, so we got it fairly cheap, but

CHAPTER 5

it's pretty much cleaned us out. We've probably got enough to buy food for today and tomorrow, but that's it. I'm going to need to earn money tonight."

"Tonight?"

"Unless you know a way of eating for free?"

Kettle on, I open the cupboards and amazingly find a box of tea bags shoved right at the back of one of them. Never in all my life has the sight of one of those little squares brought me so much joy. I'm about to mention this to Oliver when I look over and see him still staring at the coins, worry etched on his face. I bring out two mugs and put a bag in each.

"I'll get something," I tell him, as I pour the boiling water on. "I've got experience. There are plenty of places here I could work. One of those bars might need someone, even if it's just clearing glasses or washing up. I won't need to speak the language for that. There'll be something I can do."

"No," he says.

Scooping up the money and dropping it into his pocket, he stands up. Before he can leave the table, I move around to the side and block his way out.

"I am not going to stay in one room for the rest of my life, Oliver."

"I'm not asking you to do that."

"No? It feels like it."

"Really? Because to me, it feels like I'm trying to keep you safe."

He drops his head and lets out a long sigh. When he finally looks back up, his eyes are filled with the same sad expression I saw last night, only this time it doesn't disappear when he blinks.

"I don't know how to do this, Naz. I'm sorry, but I don't. Trying to keep you safe, is all I can think about. These people hunting you, they fill my nightmares. When I close my eyes, all I can see is …"

His voice fades away, but I know exactly what he was going to say. Styx. The same person that haunts my dreams, too, when they aren't filled with images of Rey or the vampire dungeon or my dad. He sighs again and shakes his head.

"I know that you're miserable, Naz. I know that *I'm* making you miserable. Shit, I'm making *myself* miserable, but you've got to bear with me. Right now, I can't relax. I can't sleep. I can't focus on anything. At this rate, even if the vampires don't find us, we'll die of starvation."

"Don't be ridiculous, Oliver. You need to let this go. I can look after myself. You don't have to worry about me."

"Yes, I do. I screwed up before. I missed the signs. I didn't see how far gone you were. If I'd realised how desperate you were about finding that damn vampire. If I'd helped you. With the Blood bank. With access to Blackwatch stuff. If I'd done any of that, then Rey might still be alive and you, you might not …" His voice fades away again.

"Might not be a werewolf?" I offer. "Oliver, I was always a wolf. It was in my genes."

"Maybe. But that doesn't mean I couldn't have stopped it from happening. I did nothing, Naz. I did nothing to protect you from that monster. And I'm sorry for how I'm acting. I just can't pretend that I'm okay with knowing you're constantly in danger."

"I told you. I can protect myself."

"Just because you're a wolf, doesn't mean you're invincible. Trust me on that."

This comment causes me to pause for a moment.

"Okay, I get it. But you must understand that you're not to blame for anything. Not Rey. Not me. It was never your job to protect us."

He nods, but it's a small gesture and I know he doesn't really believe me. A feeling of desolation hangs over us, caused by the weight of guilt that we've both been trying to shoulder for so long. In all the years I've known him, I've never seen him this bad. He's the problem solver, the one who's got a solution for everything. But right now, he looks totally defeated.

"Look, it's a nice morning. A really nice morning, by the looks of things. How about we drink our tea, then go for a walk by the river and find some breakfast? Then, if we get the feeling that this place is some secret vampire stronghold with a hundred nests and Council members lurking on every corner, then maybe I'll keep a low profile. But if it seems like it's just a regular little tourist town with miserable locals and cheap bars and you realise I'm actually completely safe and you're worrying about nothing, then maybe you could think about loosening the leash, just a little?"

He purses his lips as he considers my proposal.

"Breakfast and a walk sound good," he says. "Because there's no way I'm drinking tea here until we get some milk."

6

In the morning light, my first impressions of the town last night are confirmed. The shops and cafés that line the cobble streets are now open and bustling with people. We wander up past the bar that Oliver went into yesterday, before heading back down to take a stroll by the river. In the distance, there's a factory pumping out smoke. I idly wonder what they're making there. We come to a small park, and although the swings and slides are a little weather-beaten, there are children happily playing on them. Normality at last.

"I should probably have asked before, but where exactly are we?" I say, as we amble slowly along.

"We're in Klaipėda."

"Klaipėda. Right." I think I should have paid more attention in geography as I don't have a clue where that is. Thankfully, he realises as much from my confused expression.

"Lithuania."

"Ah. Okay."

I can't say I know where that is either, but at least I have a vague idea we're somewhere in eastern Europe.

We continue walking, occasionally stopping to admire the view. We pass one of those bridges where the railings have been covered with padlocks, the ones that people inscribe their initials on before locking them in place and throwing the keys into the river as a symbol that they will love each other forever. I can't imagine myself ever wanting to be with someone so completely that I'd use a gesture like that to show it. The cynical part of me thinks it was probably started by the owners of the nearby tourist shops to make money selling the novelty padlocks and offering engraving services.

We're now heading towards the docks. We're not talking, but at least the atmosphere is not so strained. I wouldn't go so far as to say it's pleasant but it's bearable. After a few minutes, we enter an underpass and traffic rumbles noisily above us. As we emerge on the other side, the widening river has taken on a greyish hue on its way to the sea and large barges bob up and down. In front of us is a huge area where rusty brown containers are stacked high.

"I guess we should head back, Oliver," I say, thinking it's time to buy some milk, not to mention food. When there's no reply, I turn to find him staring into the distance. I follow his gaze to where a small group of men is standing in conversation. Most likely they're dock workers having a cigarette break. They don't look any more ominous than the kids did yesterday evening, but the wolf is scraping away in my skull again. It appears that a gathering of any size is liable to set it off.

"Oliver? Shall we head back?" I say again.

"Actually, do you want to wait here a minute?"

"What? Where are you going?"

"Just wait, okay?"

He walks off towards the men, which given the lecture he gave me only the night before about moving three feet from where he was, seems very lax. I'm not going to complain, though. I watch as he approaches them.

The distance—combined with the fact I don't speak the language—means I don't have a clue what's being discussed, but I can tell by the way all eyes are on him that he's the one doing most of the speaking. After a few minutes, he turns around and strides back to me, and there's something different about him. It takes me a minute to recognise what the change is. He's actually smiling.

"Well, that's one thing sorted, then."

"What is?"

"I've got a job. I start tonight."

In celebration, we eat pastries by the river.

"What is it you'll be doing?" I ask. "They obviously didn't ask for references."

"I don't know."

"What? You must have some idea, surely?"

"Manual stuff. Lifting and loading, that sort of thing, probably. Cash in hand. Hopefully good money, too."

The cynical part of me is working overtime. This all sounds a bit too vague, dubious even. It's most unlike Oliver not to have all the facts.

"Hopefully?" I repeat. "You don't know what they're paying you?"

"We agreed to sort out the details when I get there."

I bite down on my pastry, finding it substantially drier than only a moment before. I feel he's being taken advantage of, possibly working for a small fraction of what the going rate is. But as this is the most amiable he's been in months, the last thing I want to do is ruin the atmosphere.

"Also," he says, tearing off a bit of his roll and throwing it to a couple of birds who have been creeping closer, "I think I saw a second-hand bookshop last night on the high street. We could go and have a rummage. I bet we'd find something in English. What do you say?"

It's been four hours since he left. It turns out the grotesquely floral settee is actually rather comfortable to sit on and read. We found a few classics in the shop. Jane Eyre and Dracula, not to mention Harry Potter. I'm pretty sure every second-hand bookshop in the world contains copies of that series. Oliver somehow got the owner to sell them all to us for a couple of euros which, while very cheap, cleaned us out entirely. I'm not convinced it was a good idea to spend the very last of our money like that, but Oliver was convinced tonight's work is going to pay well. Despite the fact that my eyes are drooping, and I've read this last paragraph a dozen times, I've decided to stay up until he gets back and find out how it went. What I need is something to help keep me awake. Bring on the tea bags.

Forcing myself off the sofa, I go over to the kitchen and fill the kettle. We've still got no milk, but I'm not that fussy. A well-stewed black tea should give me enough of a caffeine boost to keep me going until he returns. One good thing about not being at uni anymore, I guess, is no early morning lectures.

With the kettle boiling, I pull out one of the dining chairs and take a seat at the table. I've avoided thinking about my abandoned studies since this whole wolf thing kicked off, but now it's on my mind, I can't shift from it. I can't say that I had any firm plans after finishing my degree —finding and killing Styx was pretty much all I had on my agenda—but now what? Say that Calin manages to get Polidori to pardon me and allow me to return home. Do I just go back and carry on as if nothing ever happened? And then what? What role in life is there after uni for someone like me? If I'm truthful, given my unique experiences and talents, I'd be best off in a wolf pack. And believe me, that's a hard pill to swallow. But it would be nice to get to know Freya better.

With a click and a column of steam, the kettle informs

me it's boiled. As I get up to make my drink, there's another click as a key turns in the front door. He's back earlier than I thought he would be.

"Hang on a minute," I call, going over to take the chain off the hook. "How did it go?" I ask, opening the door, which suddenly bursts inwards as Oliver stumbles through, his legs buckling. He falls forwards and I just manage to catch him before he hits the floor. As I lower him down, I see the blood on his face. In fact, it's a bruised and battered mess. He wheezes, struggling for breath.

"What the hell happened?" I gasp, as fear grips me. "Are they here? Did the vampires find us?"

7

Thirty minutes later, this is officially the most exasperated I have ever been with anyone in my entire life. And believe me, there are some great contenders on the list. Fortunately for Oliver and any neighbours we might have, I've run out of things to yell at him. Well, almost.

"Of all the stupid, irresponsible ideas! A cage fight? Really?"

Avoiding my glare, he reaches for his cup of tea, only to wince and pull his arm back. If I was a good friend, I'd move it closer to him, but as I've already mentioned, I'm not. I'm just a seriously pissed-off one.

Abandoning the drink, he reaches into his coat pocket and pulls out a wad of notes which he slams on the table.

"Here. Take a look at that." It's the most money we've seen in a long time. "There's over two hundred Euros, Naz. Two hundred for one night's work."

"It's not one night's work if you can't move for the next two months. Your arm wasn't healed properly from what Styx did to you. How in hell's name could you think this was a plan?"

"I won, didn't I? Just like I knew I would. Besides, it looks a lot worse than it is."

He coughs and blood-tinged spittle appears at the corners of his mouth, which doesn't help his case. But I know there's nothing more I can say right now that will make any difference. I've tried to persuade him to go with me to the hospital, but he won't. He refused outright, saying he'd know if any serious damage had been done. I'm not convinced, but I'm not going to fight him right now. Someone else has done a good-enough job of that already.

"Honestly, it's not so bad," he says, aiming again for the cup of tea and this time reaching it. "Most of it's superficial. None of the guys had any training. It was all just scrapping. I had to let them get a couple of good hits in for show."

"For show? Yeah? What about this bruise here? Was that for show?"

Leaning across the table, I prod a finger into the hollow just above his collarbone, where a purple mark has already bloomed across to his shoulder. "And how about this one?" I say, and poke another. He grimaces and sucks in a lungful of air, obviously trying not to yell out in pain.

"Enough! I get your point. But you seem to be missing mine. Two hundred Euros, Naz. That will keep us going for a few weeks, easily. We can stay here or maybe find something a bit nicer. One or two evenings a month, that's all I need to do."

"There's no way you're doing this again, Oliver. Have you even looked in a mirror? I swear, you must be high or something. You look like you've done another round with Styx."

He frowns and wrinkles his nose. "It's not that bad. Besides, these things are underground, literally. They're off the radar of the authorities and the police. And before you ask, I scoured the whole place first for vamps. No sign of one."

"Because vampires wear signs?"

"You know what I mean. Give me some credit, Naz. I was at Blackwatch for a long time. I know what I'm looking for."

I'm about to reply, when something occurs to me.

"You will get back to Blackwatch, you know. When this is sorted out, I'll talk to Jessop."

"Naz, don't—"

"I mean it. He'll listen to me. When I tell him what you were doing. How you were keeping me safe."

He waves a hand to stop me, and I do, mainly because I can't stand to see the discomfort it causes.

"We can talk about that later," he says, momentarily squeezing his eyes closed against the pain. "At least we have a plan. I can fight and keep us fed. It's not ideal, I know, but it's the best we've got for now. Besides, bones heal."

"Slowly," I add, feeling he's missed a vital word. "Bones heal slowly, for you."

And just like that, the idea strikes.

"I'll do it," I say, sitting up straight. "I'll fight. Women can take part too, right?"

He shifts backwards slightly. "Women do fight."

"Then that's what I'll do."

Immediately, he's shaking his head. "The idea is that you keep a low profile, remember?"

"A moment ago, you said that these things were under the radar. Think about it. It's perfect. I heal quicker. Whatever beating I take is going to be fixed far quicker than it would be for you."

"Yes, but you seem to be forgetting a rather crucial point."

"Which is?"

"You can't fight."

The noise I make in response is somewhere between a snort and a laugh, but I feel it gets the meaning across pretty adequately.

"I can fight. I fought Styx, remember. And a whole host of other vampires. Not to mention Daniel at the wolf pack."

"Yes, but you fought them all as a wolf. Have you ever tried as a human? In a regular fist fight? A pub brawl? Even a bitch-slapping?"

"Okay, okay. I get it. But you've been telling me all along that I need to learn, and you're failing to see there's a clear solution."

"Which is?"

"You train me."

8

Talk about a full-on U-turn. After months demanding I let him teach me to defend myself and being furious at me for refusing to learn how to inflict physical pain on others, Oliver was dead set against training me. It took over forty-eight hours of solid nagging for him to agree.

"What's the difference?" I kept asking. "You wanted me to learn to fight in case I needed to protect myself."

"You were the one who told me you were done with violence. That you'd seen enough of it."

"Well maybe I was wrong. Besides, what if I do get myself in trouble again?"

With my history, I felt sure that would be a winner, but he still refused to budge.

"It'll give us something to do together," was another line I tried, when he was looking bored. All that got me was a grunt.

CHAPTER 8

"We need this." I was practically on my knees. "This is what *you* wanted. Besides, it will be good for us. A chance to have some fun." Nothing

"If I'm going to train you, we're doing it properly, Naz."

Finally!

"No messing about or treating it as a joke. If you want to learn to fight, then that means doing it right. And you'll need to get fit—running, push-ups, sit-ups, the lot."

"Fine. I will do whatever you say. But then you'll let me do these fights? Let me be the one to earn the money, rather than you risking every last bone in your body?"

"We'll see," he said eventually. "Let's see how good you are first."

Which I took as a win.

IT'S A DAY SINCE HE AGREED, AND I'M CHAMPING AT THE BIT. The wolf is not helping matters either. At least when we were staying in run-down abandoned areas, I could manage quick micro-transformations outside to keep it at bay. Yesterday, I had to do it in the living room while Oliver was in the shower. Somehow, I don't think he'd have been impressed to find a massive canine sitting on the sofa. Now he's on side to train me, we have the problem of where.

"How about in here," I say as I fix us a breakfast of

scrambled egg on toast. "I'm sure if we move the table and chairs to one side, there would be enough room."

"There wouldn't be."

"Are you sure? Maybe if we just—"

"I'm sure. We need much more space than this. You're going to have to learn to throw people, remember?"

"I am? Sure, of course I am."

"Not to mention you need a decent area to run in and perform drills."

"So where then? Down by the river? There are a couple of parks I've seen on my walks."

"Which means they're visible to the public, too. It'll have to be somewhere out of town. It'll be fine. I'll figure it out. There are woodlands all around. I just need a couple more days to rest up."

He closes his eyes and leans back into the sofa.

Mornings are the toughest for him. After lying still all night, his muscles have tightened. Watching him try to stretch them out makes me flinch, as pain flashes across his face. Today, he seems a bit better. Or rather he doesn't seem any worse, and I suppose that's something. His determination is incredible. If it was me, I'd just lie in bed moping, but he has been forcing himself to move which, I suppose, will help him heal more quickly. I expect it was the same after he took that awful battering from Styx, and I wonder if it's a Blackwatch training thing. Probably not, though. I can't imagine Rey ever being like this. She would have demanded he bring her takeaway in bed until she was better. With his shirt off, I can see that the bruises have come out fully now. I want the chance to show him, one day, how grateful I am for all he's doing for me, but I've no idea how.

"Are you okay there, staring at me?"

His voice brings me back to the moment with a jerk.

"Sorry? What? I wasn't staring."

"Yes, you were."

"No, I was just daydreaming."

"About my abs?"

"No, I was just ... just thinking, that's all."

I can feel my cheeks going red and I have absolutely no idea why, so rather than sitting here and taking any more taunts, I stand up and grab my jacket from the back of the chair.

"I'm going for a walk," I say. "Do you need anything?"

He shakes his head. "Make it a power walk, or better still, a run. You're meant to be getting fit."

"I know."

"And don't be longer than an hour or I'll start getting worried. There are clocks on buildings all around here, so there's no excuse."

"I get it, Dad."

He looks annoyed. "Don't do that. Don't act like I'm some overbearing parent. That's not fair, and you know it."

My good mood drops a fraction.

"You're right. I'm sorry. I will keep an eye on the time, and I will be back within the hour, but if I'm following instructions then so are you. Promise me you're going to rest up for the rest of the day."

"That was the plan."

"Good."

I bend down and plant a kiss on his forehead then grab a couple of notes from the jar in the cupboard. Possibly not the most secure place for our money, but opening a bank account is pretty much a no-goer at the moment. I call goodbye and head out the door.

It's only when I'm outside that I realise it's the first time I've done that—kissed Oliver in an absent-minded way—in months. It was once so natural. Maybe we're gradually finding our way back to something that resembles friendship.

Like most places, the ambiance reflects the weather, and as the sky is grey this morning, so is the town. The river, that in the sun has a hint of blue to it, is verging on sludgy brown and the buildings, despite their light stonework, all have a rather dreary aspect to them. As I reach the main street, I debate which way to go.

Power walking or running was what Oliver said I should do. But here? People obviously do run in public, but I've never felt the need. I'll probably trip over my own feet and make a fool of myself. Then again, how do you learn to do something new unless you practice? Without giving myself time to change my mind, I pick up my feet and start to jog, deciding to head away from the dock and south along the coast.

Maybe it's the wolf in me, but it feels okay. I can't keep it up for long, though. I finally settle down to the rhythm of a couple of minutes of jogging, then walking, then back to jogging, followed by walking again. (Isn't that how boy scouts are trained to run? Seems sensible to me.) Soon, I find myself at the edge of the town, and the countryside opens out. Trees and fields stretch out into the distance.

Inside me, the wolf aches to be let free. But I feel a new excitement there, too. One that's not from my inner beast. In fact, it has nothing to do with it. It's all about me.

9

"Get your elbows up! Higher! And keep them tucked closer to your body. You want to have your fists in front of your face."

"How will I see what I'm doing?"

"How big are your hands? Here. No, just stand still. Let me do it."

Coming around the side of me, Oliver shifts my elbows up and in.

I know he's struggling. How he managed to walk all the way here, I have no idea, but he was the one who wanted to do it. It cut right through me, watching him limp along and having to take all those stops, resting his hands on his knees to catch his breath. Each time, he made out there was something that had caught his eye. A boat out at sea or a bird wheeling overhead. But I get it. Pride has always been one of his weaknesses although probably his only one.

As I follow his instructions, he rests on a nearby bench,

only getting up now and then to shift my position or demonstrate a stance. But whether sitting or standing, he manages the same degree of bossiness.

"Okay, now make your fists tight," he tells me, sitting back down again. "And straighten them. Don't bend the wrists. That's a recipe for disaster. Good, and make sure your thumbs are on the outside. If you connect with them tucked in like that, you'll break them. Great. Now widen your feet a fraction more."

He's back on his feet again, this time crouching in the grass to adjust my footing.

"Not quite. You need to put that one a little further forward. Yup, that's it. Now go up on your toes more. Thinking bouncing. That's right. This is the position you need to remember. It's what we're going to keep coming back to, okay? This is your fighting stance. Got it?"

He stands up, and steps back to assess me.

Elbows in, chin down, feet together, thumbs in. Shit, that's not right. No, I can safely say I don't have it yet, although I'm definitely trying.

"So, when do I learn to actually punch?" I ask, thinking it might help my motivation if I was doing something more positive than just standing and bouncing and, all-in-all, feeling like a right prat.

"Not yet. There's no point trying that until you've improved your strength. And with that in mind, drop and give me fifty."

"Fifty?"

"Press-ups."

The only thing that drops is my jaw.

"Fifty press-ups. You are joking? The last time I tried them, I think I managed five before I fell flat on my face."

"Okay, that's a start. Do those five and then another forty-five afterwards."

He sits back on the bench and crosses his legs. A small smile twitches at the corners of his mouth.

I'm not even going to dignify that smart-ass comment with an answer. I feel my scowl says it all.

"Of course, you don't have to do this at all, if you don't want to. I saw one of the guys from the fight yesterday. They are more than happy to have me there again. I think they're pissed they lost their money last time and want the chance to back the winner."

"You are *not* fighting again. You think I didn't notice you clutching your shoulder on the way over."

"Well then, press-ups it is, I guess."

I don't get as far as fifty. I don't even get halfway, but I do pass twenty, which I'm extremely proud of, although my arms are not going to thank me tomorrow. After that, it's more drills. Pulls ups—which I can also hardly manage— sit-ups— which I can—and so many squats that my thigh muscles feel like they're on fire. After an hour, I'm certain he's about to say we've done enough for the day, but I should have known better. After all, Oliver never does anything by halves.

Balance and foot work follow. He has me shifting my weight from one foot to the other whilst ducking as he swings a stick around in an utterly reckless fashion. How he doesn't smack me in the head, I don't know. He's definitely enjoying it. Like he is when he finds a fallen tree trunk and makes me balance on it, on one foot and then the other. It leaves me wondering if I'm in a particularly twisted version of The Karate Kid meets Dirty Dancing.

At times, my mind wanders back to the pack. The last time I learned anything new outside a lecture hall was when Art and Lou taught me to block other wolves' thoughts. The other wolves that I can no longer hear and Art, who I thought was my friend but turned me over to Daniel, the biggest bully in the pack, who wanted to overthrow my mother. I don't miss that. But Lou, I do. Her endless optimism. Her constant encouragement. Even her non-stop talking. Oliver isn't quite the same with words.

"Go again," he says, when I momentarily wobble, trying to swivel on the narrowest part of the log, which is constantly rolling and threatening to pitch me off.

"I didn't fall," I object, stretching out my arms and quickly regaining my balance.

"Only because you were lucky. You need to react quicker. Go again."

There's no point in arguing, and actually, I don't want to. Whatever the state of our friendship right now, I trust that he wouldn't make me do something unless he thought it was beneficial. And I want to make him proud of me. For once.

10

Calin

"Calin, my boy, come in. Sit down. Can I get you something to drink?"

"No, thank you, sir, I'm fine."

"Very well. Shall we get straight to business then?"

It's been fourteen weeks since I left Narissa with Oliver, and until now, all my conversations with Polidori have been during meetings of the Vampire Council, so always with others present. This has been useful. The lack of focused attention on me has made it easier to hide what I can't reveal to him.

The Council itself has changed. New faces have appeared that make me feel ill at ease. They speak of humans without compassion and arrive at the gatherings reeking of fresh blood. And the sessions have become shorter and shorter. For the past three weeks, there have been none at all, which is one reason his summons came as such a surprise. That, and the location.

As long as I have been a member, Council meetings have taken place at its main place of business, an impressive former mill in the centre of the city. And yet today, I have been called to his own home, a massive four-story town house in one of the priciest locations. It's a place I know well. Throughout the years, I've enjoyed countless occasions here: parties, formal dinners, meet-and-greet cocktail events, even afternoon teas. I've mingled with high society, both vampire and human, all present at his personal invitation. But there are also darker memories.

This is where he brought me after saving my life in the First World War—after turning me. It was where I discovered what I had become and what I needed to do to survive. Here, I first drank blood, hopelessly failed to restrain myself and murdered the only humans I've ever killed. I'm reminded of this every time I walk through the doors.

Today, we're in his library, a grand room with floor to ceiling mahogany shelves. As normal, the curtains remain closed. He is sitting at his desk, a magnificent piece of French workmanship which belonged to one of the Louis. As I take a seat across from him, he pours a glass of blood from a decanter which is nearly empty. This doesn't fill me with great confidence. Polidori is well known for his restraint. But perhaps he had another guest before me.

"You will excuse me for arranging to meet here today," he says. "You may have noticed that change is afoot in the Council."

"You mean the new members?"

"Amongst other things. Have you had the chance to introduce yourself to them properly?"

"No. Not yet. You know what it's like. Always the best intentions, but then time somehow runs away with you."

"Indeed. Indeed."

Fortunately, I've always been enough of a recluse when it comes to mixing with other vampires that he shouldn't think this is anything out of the ordinary. But I worry that he may suspect that I'm lying or obfuscating, at best.

There's something strange about these two new ones. I noticed it the first time I met them. It was the way they seemed to find it impossible to sit still, their hands constantly going to their chins. This is usually the behaviour of new vampires who have only recently had their bottom fangs removed. But if that is the case, how have they attained membership of the Council? No one is ever invited to join until they have had the time to show themselves to be pillars of the community—reliable, trustworthy and cognisant of the delicate balance between us and humans. Not that Styx met those criteria, however. Right now, I'm starting to wonder who does.

"Vegan dogs."

CHAPTER 10

"Vegan dogs?" I repeat, sure I must have misheard him.

"Indeed. Humans, despite the true nature of their canine companions, have taken it upon themselves to force their trendy eating habits upon their poor pets. Cats too, I believe. Were you aware of this?"

"No, I don't think so."

While I'm utterly confused why a conversation between us would start in this manner, Polidori simply nods, knowledgeably.

"Tell me, Calin, do you think these animals will thrive on such a diet?"

There is clearly only one answer that he expects.

"I cannot say. Although, it seems unlikely."

"It does, doesn't it?" He pauses as if contemplating this. "I will not lie to you, Calin. I have said it before, and I will say it again, I believe that there are forces at play. Change is on the horizon. An unprovoked witch attack in one of our places of sanctuary and a Council member murdered by a werewolf are signs, Calin. Signs of trouble ahead. And we need to do everything in our power to stop it, to quash it before it can gain any traction."

This is like a stake to the gut. I was hoping that by now he would be open to discuss what happened to Styx, and Narissa's involvement, but obviously, that is not the case.

"I have been in talks with one of the wolf packs, South Pack. They have agreed to support us should any further problems arise for us with witches."

"Support us?"

"In hunting, finding and eradicating them."

I feel as if all the air has been sucked out of the room. Witches are humans, in fact some of the wisest and most compassionate to walk the Earth. Yes, they used to kill vampires, but considering what vampires did to them, that's unsurprising. To actively hunt them down because of one incident and with no evidence of their complicity in anything else untoward, seems to go against everything we stand for.

I try to hide my shock but fail, and a sad smile forms on Polidori's lips.

"You are a gentle soul, Calin, you always have been. It is why I chose you, after all, not only to become one of us but also to join me in the inner circle of the Council. But we must not let our sensitivities overshadow the bigger picture."

What is *the bigger picture?* part of me would like to ask. The other part isn't sure it could stomach the answer. Instead, I go down what I hope is a more diplomatic route.

"Do many witches even still exist?" I ask. "Surely there can't be many. Added to which, the grimoires have been in our possession for a very long time, and without them, they're not powerful enough to be of any risk to us."

"I would like to think you're right. Possibly you are, but we just don't know, and I can't take any chances. As vampires, we are safe hunting for them in urban areas, but it's likely that any remaining covens will have taken refuge in out-of-the-way places, much as our wolf pack friends have. With their ability to cover large rural areas, the wolves are going to set about searching for them. The sooner we nip this in the bud, the better."

Werewolves siding with vampires to track down witches. I'll be the first to admit that what I am doesn't come under the heading of "natural", but this feels ... almost barbaric. A literal witch hunt.

"The South Pack, you say. And what about the North Pack?"

With a slow sigh, he reaches for the decanter and fills up his glass again. The Polidori I knew would make that quantity last a full day. Now he's getting through it in less than ten minutes.

"Yes, I'm glad you have brought them up. There has been some recent, shall we say, restructuring in leadership there and many of them have felt it wise to join their brothers and sisters in the south, to help with our cause, but there remains a core of resistance. I have also learned that it was a member of their pack who was responsible for Damien's murder."

"Really?"

"Yes. The daughter of the Alpha, no less. Or should I say, former Alpha. As long as that particular young wolf is allowed to live, she will be a rallying point for the rebels, who will, no doubt, form some kind of resistance around her. There may not be many of them, but they could certainly cause us some inconvenience."

The smell of his bloody refreshment suddenly becomes overwhelming and my gut starts to churn. Never, since my first days in this house, have I been so desperate to run from it. I need to get out of this room and onto the open road. Even in the midday sun.

"So, what is it you want me to do?" I ask him, already fearing I know the answer.

"I need you to find that wolf," he says. "I need you to find her and kill her."

11

Narissa

"Keep your back straight when you duck. You have to spring back after the attack as quickly as possible. That's it. Much better. Now, go again. Switch it up. Go for the uppercut combination."

For three weeks, this has been our daily routine, with every minute focused on fighting and fitness, and I'm not ashamed to say, I'm pretty impressed with how well I've done. Oliver seems to be, too.

"That's good. Better than last week, that's for sure. And I can't believe there's barely a mark where I hit you yesterday. Sorry about that again by the way."

"It's fine. Like you said, I've got to learn to take a real punch. And I heal fast."

"You seriously do. There's barely a bruise."

There is a bruise, though. I'd heal a hell of a lot faster if I became the wolf for longer than the transformations I've been making, which I've kept as brief as possible. Just enough to check I'm still in control. Interestingly, I can go for longer periods without feeling the need to change. In the past three weeks, I've done it less than a dozen times, normally during training in the forest where no one's going to run into us. I've taken myself off for five minutes, far enough that Oliver can't see, normally with the excuse that nature's calling. Which, in a manner of speaking, it is. Just not the way it does for most people.

I know the wolf wants more. I can feel it yearning to be set free. It wants to run through the trees, feel the grass beneath its paws. But at the same time, there seems to be a level of respect growing for the human part of me. I suppose if I did just heal as a wolf every time I get a solid whack, there'd be less incentive to improve. I figure that a few sparring bruises will serve as a reminder to get better faster. While I'm a long way from professional standard, I believe I'm beginning to hold my own well enough to get through at least a couple of rounds of prize fighting, and fingers crossed, Oliver thinks so, too.

"You've got two major advantages when it comes to fighting. Number one: your pain threshold is insanely high. That's immediately going to freak out your opponents. Number two: your stamina's really good now; you shouldn't have any problem outlasting them. You just have to make sure you get some good strong blows in and don't make any stupid mistakes. Your balance is still shocking, though. You need to work on that."

"I think shocking is a bit harsh."

"Abysmal, then. Is that better?"

"Hey!" I land a punch on his shoulder which lands far harder than I intended. It causes him to flinch, in what I hope is pain rather than surprise.

"You really want to start a fight with me now?" he smirks, grabbing me by the wrist.

"I think I'd give you a run for your money."

"Is that right?"

"Come on, then."

I twist out of his grip and start bouncing on my toes, the way he taught me, bobbing back and forth, not giving him a stationary target.

As much as learning to fight like this has been to win us some money, even if I don't earn a penny, I feel it's been worth it for this. Us. Oliver and me. The change in our relationship the last few weeks has been like coming up for air when you're drowning. Oddly, we still have our moments, when it seems like he can't bear to look at me, but they're fewer and farther between now. We've been joking more. Laughing together. Last night, when I was reading another of the paperbacks we found in the second-hand bookshop, I ended up lying with my head on his lap. I did it completely absentmindedly. It was the type of thing we'd have done quite naturally in the days before everything went to shit. When I realised what I'd done, I thought he would find some excuse to get up and leave, but he didn't. We just stayed there, the pair of us, like it always used to be.

"Don't get predictable," he says, jabbing towards my jaw. "Keep mixing it up. You have legs too, you know. You can use them."

"Like this?" I ask, leaning back and swinging a kick at his side. I thought it was going to be a pretty good strike, and it might have been had he not intercepted it. Instead, I'm left hopping on one foot, thrashing around while he holds the other in the air with a massive grin on his face.

"I think you should probably avoid getting too cocky," he laughs.

He drops my leg, grabs a drink of water and then picks up his bag.

"Come on. Let's head back. I'm pretty sure it's your turn to cook."

"It is absolutely not. I made us cheese sandwiches last night."

"That doesn't count as cooking."

"Of course, it does."

"You didn't cook anything. The clue is in the word, 'cook'."

I bump him with my hip as we fall into stride next to each other.

"You really want me to? I can do that if you want. What do you fancy? You name it, I'll make it. How about lasagne? I made one once, remember?"

He pulls a face, which I deserve considering the disaster that meal was. Uncooked pasta, yet over-cooked meat.

Even Rey couldn't finish it, and she would eat almost anything.

"I think we'd be better off if you stick to sandwiches. I don't want to risk food poisoning."

It doesn't take long until we're out of the forest and heading in the direction of the factory chimneys and civilisation. It's early evening, but the sun is still quite high in the sky. The days are getting longer. When we reach the edge of town, there's a man sitting on a bench. He's of similar age to us and vaguely familiar. Possibly, I think, one of the men we saw at the dock when Oliver arranged to fight. My suspicions are confirmed when he waves him over to talk.

A flurry of nerves builds inside me, but also a tinge of excitement. Our pot of money is still okay—whilst not a culinary delight, my sandwiches are pretty budget friendly—but it's not going to last forever. If we get the chance to win some more, or more specifically *I* get the chance, then I think we should go for it. I try to listen in, but I can't make out what's being said. Anyway, the only Lithuanian I have mastered so far is prašom and ačiū.

"So?" I ask Oliver when he returns to me. "It's another fight, isn't it? Can I do it this time? I know you don't think I'm ready yet, but I am. When did he say it would be?" Jeez, I sound like Lou, with all the endless questions.

Whether it's to deliberately annoy me or not, Oliver walks at least ten paces before speaking.

"It's another fight," he says.

"And when?"

"Tonight."

My heart does a flip. "What did you say? Did you say yes? Did you say I'd fight?"

He continues walking without answering, finally turning to me and coming to a halt just before the padlock bridge. "I told him I wasn't up for another just yet," he says.

"But—"

"But I said I would bring him someone who was."

12

I am *so* excited. Seriously pumped. Never in my life would I have imagined that entering some dodgy cage fight would be my idea of fun, yet I am happy to admit that I am buzzing.

"Remember, the aim of today isn't to win. I'm not expecting that, and you shouldn't, either. This is just a practice run. An opportunity to see what it's like to fight against someone who isn't there to go easy on you. You'll probably get hurt."

"I understand. I do."

"And remember what I said about staying close to me and not drawing attention to yourself. You fight when it's your turn, and the rest of the time, you keep a low profile. There were no vampires around the last time I was there, but that doesn't mean we can take any risks.

"Concentrate on what I've taught you and observe your opponent's technique. Check which side they favour. Look for any weak spots. I didn't win last time by being the strongest. I did it by watching and memorising their habits. You must do the same."

We walk across the open dock area until we reach the stacks of rusting containers. I follow Oliver into the maze of metal. After a few minutes, however, I begin to grow concerned.

"Are you sure we're not lost?" I ask, as we travel deeper into the shadows. I can just about make him out, shaking his head.

"There are marks on the corners. See?" He indicates an etching on one, at eye level. I wouldn't have noticed it had he not pointed it out, but now I know what to look for, they're pretty easy to spot.

"It should be just up here."

"Really, I can't hear anything."

"No, you wouldn't. It's underground, remember?"

I freeze, paralysed by the images that surge through my mind.

"Naz, are you okay?"

I shake my head, trembling now.

"Underground? You never said anything about that"

"Yes, I did. I'm sure I did."

"I thought you meant underground as in a low-key, secret kind of way. Not actually *underground*."

"It's both. Why, you're not claustrophobic, are you? It's a massive space down there. I'll be with you the whole time."

"It's not that."

CHAPTER 12

"Then what?"

I feel panic building as I remember the Blood Bank which, just like this place, was subterranean. I asked her to leave me. I told her to go, and I thought she had. But she hadn't and my best friend died there trying to protect me. I'm nearly choking on my tears now.

"Rey," I finally cough out. "The Blood Bank."

Realisation suddenly dawns on him, followed by a look somewhere between horror and pity.

"I didn't think, Naz. I'm so sorry. We don't have to do this." He takes my hand. "Come on."

As he moves to guide me back the way we came, I remain rooted to the spot.

"I can do it." I drop his hand and nod as confidently as I can manage. "Let's go. I can still fight."

"Naz, you don't have to."

"I know I don't. But I want to. I've been training and I'm not giving up now. Please."

He looks at me for a few seconds, perhaps giving me the chance to change my mind.

"I will be with you the entire time, remember," he says, at last. "And if when you get down there, you want to leave, that's fine. Just say. But they're only people, Naz, that's all. Only people."

One more turn and we reach the entrance to a staircase. As much as I try to block out all thoughts and images of the Blood Bank, it's not easy. This reminds me of it so much. The narrows stairs, the grimy handrail, the noise that gets louder the lower we descend. I close my eyes and grip Oliver's hand tightly, as he guides me down.

In the back of my head, the wolf is on high alert, snarling and snapping, ready to pounce at any moment.

I keep telling myself that this isn't the same as when I couldn't save Rey. At the Blood Bank, I was human. I'm not just that anymore. I'm not weak now.

We've got this, I say to myself and the wolf. *We'll be fine. There's nothing here to be afraid of. They're only people. Only people.*

When we reach the bottom of the stairs, Oliver pushes open the door and light floods out. This, I discover, is nothing like the Blood Bank.

13

It's hard to believe it's been kept a secret. I'm not sure what I was expecting but nothing as professional and large scale as this. The space is cavernous with gantries running along the walls. Powerful spotlights on heavy chains are suspended from the ceiling, illuminating a full-size boxing ring but with an iron cage built around it. It seems to only have one door. An impressive speaker system is pounding out techno music. Whoever organises this takes it all very seriously.

"Where are we?" I ask, trying to make sense of all the space. "Surely it isn't part of the docks?"

"No, I don't think so," Oliver replies. "From what I gather, this is where they built their first steel works in the 1850s. Then, when the town grew and they needed more space for the port in the 1940s, they moved the factory over to the other side of the river. Most of the buildings were demolished, but only ever to surface level. They didn't need to do more to accommodate all the containers, so they left it at that. Hence all this space down below. Apparently, there are some old furnaces, too, although I don't know where."

"How did you learn all that?"

"I was just chatting with a couple of blokes the last time I was here."

"Was that before or after you got beaten up?"

"Hey, I won, remember? You should have seen the other guys."

As always, I'm in awe of how he discovers stuff like this —it's probably down to his Blackwatch training—but I'm too distracted trying to take in my surroundings to ask more questions.

At a rough guess, there are about a hundred people present. Most of them are sitting on chairs around the ring or standing on the gantries looking down. In the cage, two men are circling one another. Both are large, but in a more middle-aged-spread kind of way, as opposed to toned and muscular. If this is the standard of fighter Oliver went up against, I'm not surprised he won.

As we move further in, there's a murmuring and exchange of glances, both from the floor and up in the gantries, too. Even the guy in charge of the music is staring at us. It's hard not to feel uncomfortable, even when I know the attention isn't on me.

"You obviously made quite an impression the last time you were here," I whisper. "They don't look particularly pleased to see you."

CHAPTER 13

"No, I think I may have taken out their local favourite."

The fans switch their attention back to the fight, as a flurry of punching and pushing sees one of the men ending up with his face pressed into the bars. His opponent grabs him by the hair, pulls his head back and then slams it into the ironwork again. The crowd is on its feet, cheering and baying for blood. There's certainly plenty of that. The action lacks the finesse of a boxing match. It's far more brutal and raw. The referee seems in no rush to intervene, even though the guy can barely see through his swollen eyes and probably can't breathe anymore through his smashed-up nose. With a final elbow to the top of the head, he collapses unconscious on the canvas. The referee finally steps in and declares the winner, holding his bloody hand aloft.

I look at Oliver. He shrugs.

The victor bursts through the door of the cage to the cheers of his friends and supporters, while two burly guys half carry, half drag the other man out.

"Are you okay?" Oliver asks.

I just nod. I can't think of anything to say.

We find seats, ready for the next bout. Two women now enter the ring. One is dressed in a crop top and loose black shorts, with tightly braided hair. The other has a shaved head. Her attire is much the same, just in yellow rather than black. I look down at my jeans and baggy t-shirt and feel maybe I missed the memo about the dress code. Not much I can do about it now, so I focus on what I can, which is learn.

Paying close attention, I try to identify a pattern to the women's movements, although they seem to consist mainly of bobbing and weaving. I can feel Oliver watching me as I study them, no doubt ready to answer any questions I might have, but for now, there aren't any. I'm doing exactly what he told me to do. Watch.

Already, I can tell Braids is the stronger of the two. She's not throwing as many punches—hardly any, in fact—but every time she does land one, it rocks the other girl. Skinhead is ducking and diving, trying to stay clear of her fists, occasionally throwing out a speculative kick when she gets the chance. But inch by inch, Braids is forcing her to back-peddle towards the cage wall. Skinhead lashes out once more with her foot in a last-ditch attempt to open up some space, but Braids catches her ankle and upends her. As they crash to the floor, Braids is quickly astride her opponent who is flailing ineffectually with her legs and desperately trying to cover her face with her arms as the blows rain down on her head.

"Surely she's going to give up soon?" I hiss to Oliver. "She's going to get killed, otherwise."

"It's harder to admit defeat when you're in there than you'd think from here," he responds.

It must be true as, despite her obviously hopeless situation, skinhead continues to battle on, trying to claw her way free. Finally, Braids manages to pin one of her arms with her left hand, leaving her exposed to the full force of her right.

The referee reaches over, pulls her off her stricken opponent and raises her hand.

"Not a bad fight," Oliver says.

"Not bad? That bald girl was thrashed."

"Yes, but I bet she held out for far longer than people expected her to. Besides I suspect, like you, she was here to learn as much as to win. She'll improve. Just lacks a bit of strength and confidence. That said, letting herself get backed onto the bars like that was a rookie mistake. She should have kept moving around. Kept side-stepping."

Braids is bouncing around the ring triumphant, arms pumping the air, but my eyes return to the loser, as I try to digest everything that Oliver just told me.

She sure looks strong enough as she rolls over and pushes herself to her knees, streams of sweat and blood weaving down her forehead. Her skin is glistening, her chest heaving and there's a look of deep anger on her face. Maybe she had come here to learn, like Oliver suggested, but from her expression, it's clear that she's not at all happy to do that by losing. After a moment, she regathers herself and heads to the cage door, at which point Oliver turns back to me.

"Right. Are you ready then?"

"For what?"

"To fight."

14

I don't know why the hell I was so excited before. I'm not now. I'm close to crapping myself. Oliver has spent the last half hour chatting to the organisers and various other shady looking people. The result is that I'm currently standing in the cage, in my T-shirt and jeans, waiting to have the shit beaten out of me, which shouldn't be difficult—see previous comment. On the plus side, my opponent looks far less professional than the women we watched earlier. Like me, she's dressed in more casual attire, her tight vest top exposing cheap-looking tattoos. Her hair is bright pink, and she has a wild look in her eyes.

"Sure you want to do this?" Oliver asks, through the bars.

"I'm sure," my damn mouth replies before my brain kicks in. Or maybe it was the wolf part of it that answered. It's been buzzing away quietly since we arrived. I'd almost

CHAPTER 14

forgotten it was there, it's been so quiet lately. But not now. Now, it's excited. Unlike me.

God damn it, Naz, get yourself together. You want to do this. This is what you've been practising for, after all.

I know I've been training for weeks, but now it seems all too real. Feet together, or was it apart? And where the hell is my thumb supposed to go, again? Shit, it's like my grey matter has just turned to jelly.

"She's your perfect first opponent," Oliver says encouragingly. "She seems inexperienced and doesn't look that light on her feet, either. Plus, she won't have your pain threshold."

"Have you seen those tattoos?" I ask. "I don't think a person who can handle something like that is worried about discomfort."

He doesn't even glance over at her as he continues his pep talk.

"It's about learning, remember. Practice, not perfection. Now go give it your best shot. And remember, you have the advantage of being you-know-what."

"That's only an advantage if I change mid ring and rip her throat out," I hiss back.

"Okay, don't do that. Definitely don't do that."

For the first time since I stepped into the cage, a shadow of worry flashes across his face.

"You're not going to do that, are you?"

"No, of course I'm not."

"You're sure?"

I glower at him.

He looks me up and down and purses his lips in a way that doesn't fill me with confidence.

"What? What is it?"

"Your T-shirt. It's too baggy. It'll gives her something to catch hold of and control you. You'd be better off removing it."

"What and give you and everyone else the opportunity to perve at me in my bra?"

"Please, you were hardly shy when you used to waltz around my flat in your underwear the last umpteen years. Seriously though, there are no rules. The ref isn't going to stop her if she uses it to her advantage. Think about it."

I do but only momentarily, before shaking my head.

"It's fine. She'd have to get close to me to grab it, and I have no intention of letting that happen."

"Okay. Your decision."

A minute later, the ref yells, and I'm suddenly standing in the middle of the ring, with Oliver's voice fading into the distance.

Close up, the girl's not half as fragile as she looked before. Her arms are rippling with muscle, and she stands a good six inches taller than me.

I'm still considering this when a bell rings and my opponent's fist flies out and strikes my square in the jaw. Stumbling back, I shake my head, trying to figure out what just happened, only to see her fist coming towards me once more. This time, I'm ready, and I dodge to the side before she can hit me again.

In terms of sportsmanship, I'm not impressed. Seri-

CHAPTER 14

ously, give a girl a chance to get her bearings before you start with that. Unfortunately, I'm not able to take it up with her or even dwell on the matter for long, because her fists are still flying. And not just her fists. Her feet and knees, too. I just don't have enough limbs to block all the different angles that she's coming from.

So much for not being light on her feet. Right now, she looks like a bloody gazelle. It's not like the blows hurt that much, compared to the ones Oliver has dealt out recently. They have more of an annoying-mosquito quality to them rather than huge strength behind them. But mosquitos can bite.

"Go on the offensive!" Oliver's yell makes its way through the fog of my thoughts. "Use your jab! You've got this Naz! You've got this!"

This is a learning exercise, I remind myself, as I take another punch in the guts. *So learn. And get one good punch in, at least.*

With renewed determination, I drive myself forwards, lunging at her with the first real show of aggression since the fight started.

She blocks my strike, but it slows her down.

"Yes Naz! That's it! And again! Go again!"

Oliver's voice spurs me on and I lash out again, but connect with nothing but air. I swing at her for a third time, certain that I'm going to connect, when there's a tightening around my back and shoulders and I'm dragged forwards, my breath catching in my lungs. I look down. She has the front of my T-shirt in one hand and is yanking me further towards her while thumping me in the side with the other.

"Hey!" I yell, pulling back to try and get out of her grip, but her nails are in there tight, and I can't get away from her. She lands another punch and then kicks my legs, causing me to stumble. I try to regain my balance, but she uses my shirt to swing me around and send me sprawling onto the deck. In a flash, she's on top of me and her forearm is crushing my windpipe, her sweaty face just inches from mine.

"Baggy T-shirt," she says in a thick accent, and smiles. "Rookie mistake."

And that's when the wolf joins in.

15

It's like a switch going off in my head but not to change me into the wolf this time. I'm still in charge of that. It's doing something different, taking control of something else. The instinct to survive. To fight.

I buck hard beneath her and pitch her forward over my head. Quickly rolling onto my stomach, I jump on her back before she's had the chance to turn around. She uses her considerable strength to lift us both and stands. Still holding onto her upper body, I use my feet to kick her legs away from under her, sending her face first into the mat again. I start to rain blows down and she curls up, covering her head. A moment later and the referee is pulling me off and lifting my arm to declare me the winner.

"Yes! Naz! Wow!" Oliver comes bounding into the cage and hugs me off my feet. "How? How on earth? Where did that come from?"

"I guess I had a good coach."

"No, I did *not* teach you that. Trust me, I would have remembered. Come on. Let's get you some water."

While the shock of what I just did is still uppermost in my brain, he leads me over to one of the benches, fetches a bottle of water and forces me to drink it.

"So, what was all that at the beginning? Were you just bluffing? Trying to make her think she had you?"

"No, I don't think so. I don't really know. When she pinned me down, something just clicked into place."

I consider mentioning the wolf, but I'm not sure myself how it happened. I didn't become the wolf. It was more like it became part of me.

"Well, do you think you can get it to click into place a little sooner next time? But that … that was incredible."

It's wonderful to see his face lit up like this. I can't remember him looking so excited about anything in the longest time and the return of that inane grin causes a whole heap of warmth to flood through me.

"So, how shall we celebrate?" he asks. "What do you want to do?"

I hesitate and look back at the cage, before turning to him with the most restrained grin I can manage.

"I want to go again," I say.

THE ORGANISERS WERE ALL TOO KEEN TO SEE ME IN THE ring again. It took a couple of minutes for the wolf to decide to join in during the second fight. I was hoping I'd be able to tap into it immediately, but it turned out it would take a string of hard punches to my ribs for it to show up and offer me its support. Those ribs are now on open display, since I ripped the bottom off my T-shirt and converted it into a makeshift crop top. Oliver was right, it's better this way, but it doesn't look anywhere near as sporty or professional as the other women fighters.

I'm currently up against Braids. I've defeated two opponents so far this evening, but she is far superior to them. There's a fluidity to her movements that makes it harder to anticipate where she's going to strike next. Harder, that is, unless the wolf is helping. After the first few strikes, it already knows how she's going to move. It's like the very first time I ran in the forest. Back then, smells and sights were stored away for future reference. Here, it's the twitch of a muscle, or the curl of a finger.

"Keep your feet moving!" Oliver shouts over the noise of the crowd. "You've got this!"

Various cheers and boos echo around the room. They're certainly paying attention to this fight, which I'm confident I'm going to win. Part of me feels bad for the girl. She must have trained for years to be this good. Her technique is exceptional, far better than mine. And she's clearly as strong as hell. She's just at the distinct disadvantage of not having werewolf DNA in her makeup. However, I came here for a reason, to win and earn money, and I'm not going to let a small thing like that make me feel guilty.

As she throws her next punch, I block it with my elbow,

only to swing around and bring the other one down on her shoulder. Her knees buckle and she drops. People are stamping their feet and cheering. You know, for someone who's shied away from being the centre of attention her whole life, this is something I could get used to.

As my arm is lifted into the air for the third time, Oliver rushes in to join me again.

"That was great! You are officially incredible!" He nods to his hand and the thick wad of notes he's holding. "How about we call it a night now?"

"Is that it? Is there no one else I can fight?"

"I haven't asked. It's better to quit now, while you're still feeling reasonably okay. Believe me, tomorrow your muscles are going to hurt. Let's head back and get pizza on the way. I think it's fair to say you've earned it."

I glance down at the scrapes and bruises I've collected and it's clear he's right. Despite the fact that I've won all my bouts, I've taken a good few hits, too. But while the idea of pizza is very tempting, adrenaline is still coursing through me. Another fight would help me hone my skills even further. Besides, although I know I'm going to be sore tomorrow, it's not like I'll hurt the way the average person would. I've got werewolf DNA to help me. A long soak in the tub and some stretching will be all it takes to have me feeling on top form again.

"Maybe just one more fight?" I suggest.

"I don't think you should."

"I'll win."

CHAPTER 15

"It's not about that." He clenches his jaw and takes a deep breath before looking around us.

"We're meant to be keeping a low profile, remember? With your unexpected winning spree, you've already drawn enough attention to yourself tonight."

"It can't be any more than you did."

"True, but that still doesn't make it right."

As much as I hate to admit it, I'm beginning to agree that calling it a night is probably the most sensible idea. I can still think rationally. The wolf isn't in control of me. A further week's training with Oliver will keep it happy and me motivated.

"Look, we've earned good money," he says. You've found your rhythm. If you want to fight again, we can arrange it. We'll come back in a month or so."

"A month? We might not even be here that long. How about a week?"

He hesitates.

"Two weeks."

"One. Oliver, trust me. I have this. Besides, if we do have to move on soon, one week and a big win will set us up. I know I'll be able to beat whoever I face. You do, too."

"Fine," he agrees with a mock groan. "One week and you can go again."

16

Calin

I've kept moving. That way at least it appears I'm doing what Polidori asked of me—hunting down Narissa. Of course, I don't need to. I've known where she is every day since she left the wolf pack. My check-ins with Oliver have been less frequent than I would have liked, but I know she's safe and that's all that matters. He's teaching her to fight, too, he says. That's a sensible idea. One I should have probably considered, although she already had enough on her plate before, plus dealing with me.

It's hard not to let emotions get the better of me. Part of me wants nothing more than to go Europe and run away with her myself. But then we'd both be at risk and Polidori would have a bigger target to aim at.

CHAPTER 16

I've been travelling around the UK. Nowhere in particular, just enough to appear that I'm searching for her. I've been making my presence known, dropping in on Blackwatch in various cities, showing my face at a few of our feeding haunts, making it look like I'm busy. But now I'm back in the last place I saw her—Scotland, heading to where the wolf pack used to live.

A fog sits low in the valley as I drive in and park up. Although it's only been a few months since the attack, the place has an air of neglect, almost sadness. The thick mist has all but blotted out the sun, but old habits die hard and I pull on my jacket and hat before getting out.

I can hear there's no one in the village. There could be some wolves deep in the forest, but none close enough for me to be aware of. I really don't know why I've come here. I consider getting back in the car and leaving. I could spend a month in France. Say I heard a rumour about her being there. I could make up something plausible. I've got a good friend in north of Montpellier, Régine, a human that I've known since she was a child. She'd shelter me indefinitely if I asked her. But instead, I start walking, and my feet lead me towards the cabin that Narissa and I shared.

I push open the door and step inside. A rush of our mingled scents immediately hits me. How did I resist her for so long? How did I manage to control myself after that first taste? Maybe it was the werewolf gene in her blood. Or perhaps that was what I found so compelling in the first place. But it's not the only thing I miss. It's all of her. Her dry, self-deprecating humour. Her rash, emotional outbursts.

The curtains are closed and only a little light filters past them into the room, yet it is clear to see that nothing has changed. Her father's diaries are still sitting in their boxes. Obviously, the vampires who raided the place didn't know their significance. I have no doubt, with all those years of experiences contained within, they'd make for interesting reading. I stoop and pick one up at random. I'm about to open it when a noise renders me frozen to the spot. A deep, guttural growl. I turn around slowly, lifting my hands—one still gripping the book— high above my head as a sign I'm no threat. Fear churns in my stomach.

In the doorway is a huge, red-brown animal with deep blue eyes. It snarls and snaps, teeth bared at me. I've never gone one-on-one against a werewolf before, but having seen Narissa in action, I can say with some certainty that it's not something I ever want to try. Backing away, hands still raised, I hope my intentions are clear.

"That's enough. Stop it." Chrissie pushes past it and into the cabin. A moment later, the wolf is gone, replaced by her human alter ego. Lou looks no happier to see me now than she did a moment ago. I begin to think it was a mistake coming back.

"Calin. What are you doing here? Do you have news?"

She looks at me expectantly, eyes full of hope, making it all the worse when I shake my head.

"No. Nothing good. Polidori has tasked me with finding Narissa. Bringing her back to the Council."

"But you won't, will you?" Lou steps in front of her mother. "You can't. You mustn't let them know about her."

"He already knows what she is and what she did. We can assume Juliette supplied him with all the details. But she's safe, for now. What about here? What about the pack?"

"What pack?" Lou demands. I hope she's just being facetious, but when I look at Chrissie, the pain in her face confirms the truth.

"There are only a few of us left. A couple of dozen, but that's it," the older woman says.

"Where are the rest? Surely they didn't all follow Juliette?"

"She didn't give them much choice. Let's just say her methods of persuasion were highly effective."

"She came back a couple of weeks after Freya's funeral," Lou explains. "Most of us had managed to regroup. We thought it would be safe by then. But she arrived with her betas and killed four of our gammas—four of my friends." She looks at her feet. "There was no reason for it. It was just a show of strength. She said that she would return with more of her pack and kill anyone who didn't immediately leave with her. We had two choices: join her or flee. The cowards joined her."

"They weren't cowards, Lou. They were scared."

She ignores her mother. "Art went with her, of course. He makes me sick to my stomach."

"Is there no one who can challenge her? No one to act as Alpha for this reduced pack," I ask.

A new sadness falls upon the women.

"I am not strong enough," Chrissie says, sadly. "I wish I were. But I was never meant to lead. What remains can barely be called a pack at all. I can guide them for the time being, but eventually ..."

In a moment of tenderness, Lou places her hand on her mother's shoulder.

"It'll take time," she says. "Those of us who are left, are strong. We will challenge her one day. We are not ready yet, but we'll get there. Besides, we have Adam."

"Adam?" I ask.

Chrissie shoots her daughter a look, indicting she's said too much, but if she doesn't trust me by now, something's very wrong.

"Adam was one of ours. He *is* one of ours. He was very close to Freya. In fact, he would have been one of her betas if he'd felt ready for the role. He's gone over to Juliette's side to feed us information."

"Has he managed that? Does he know what their plan is?"

"No. She's a master of secrecy. She keeps everything close to her chest. But he says that vampires have been regularly visiting the pack. The place stank of them when he arrived, too. They're sending wolves out."

"Sending them out where?"

"We don't know. There's a chance they're hunting Narissa. Juliette was fearful of Freya's strength. She will see Narissa as a threat. The same way that Daniel did. She will want her dead."

17

Narissa

It's safe to say I hurt more than I expected. A lot more. Oliver was right. I've woken up to pain in muscles I didn't even know I had. My back and shoulders feel like they've been replaced by steel girders, refusing to stretch or flex, and every time I go to bend my knees, I feel I've aged seventy years.

"You should have had an ice bath last night," he says, regarding me with a smirk.

"That sounds like the most unappealing thing ever."

"More unappealing than this?"

"It'll be fine. I'm just going to lie here for a week. Can you pass my book over?"

As I reach out to take it from him, my neck goes into spasm. This is not good.

"Jeez." I wince and rub the top of my spine. "Tell me we have some painkillers somewhere?"

His eyes narrow.

"What?"

"You've never hurt like this before."

"Well, I've never fought like that before."

"You think I didn't notice? Why was that?"

"I don't know." I shrug and even that little movement makes me grimace.

"I guess it was the adrenaline of a real fight." I try to sound nonchalant.

"Really, that's all it was?"

"Why? What else would it be?"

"I don't know. You tell me?"

For a moment, I'm tempted to make light of it again and tell him he's over-thinking this, but lying to Oliver only ever lands me in deep water, plus I've already promised myself I'm not going to do it anymore. The thing is, it's difficult to understand, let alone explain.

"I feel like maybe the wolf helped me out a bit."

"The wolf helped you out? What does that even mean?"

"I'm not sure. I guess it put me in a more aggressive mindset, got to me to focus, see things clearer and anticipate what my opponent was going to do."

I finish my rubbish explanation, expecting him to say

something at best cynical and at worst rude. But instead, he just nods.

"I suppose that makes sense. Although I don't know why you always refer to it in the third person. You are the wolf, aren't you?"

That's a question I've often asked myself and one I don't yet feel I have an answer to.

"It's so difficult to explain. I'm the wolf when I turn into it, but the rest of the time, I'm the old me and it's just lurking in the background, biding its time. Can we not talk about this right now? I can't think straight. I need to sleep. For a week."

"Oh no, you don't," he says, reaching down, grabbing my wrists and pulling me up.

"Stop it! What do you think you're doing?"

"You need to keep moving. You think it's bad now. If you just lie here, those muscles are going to seize up completely and you'll have weeks of pain ahead of you."

"I'm not sure I can even stand up straight," I complain.

"And you need to get back into training. Assuming you want to fight again."

It's a tough call, but yes, I do.

"We'll start with just walking," he says. "We'll only go as far as the forest. By the time we get there, you'll feel a lot looser. Trust me."

HE LIED. I DON'T FEEL EVEN A LITTLE BIT BETTER. IN FACT, I feel worse. It's gone from soreness and dull aches to searing pain, not to mention a headache that's pounding through my skull with every step I take. And it's not just me that's feeling it. For the last thirty minutes, there's been a whimpering in the back of my head that's growing louder. Whatever I did last night invoking the wolf to help me fight, it's clearly something my body doesn't approve of. Hybridising my two personas is obviously not ideal.

"Maybe you should sit down for a while," Oliver suggests when we reach a tree stump at the edge of the forest. "What about water? Have you drunk enough?"

"I don't think this is a simple dehydration issue."

"I don't get it. I thought you'd heal faster."

My mind flashes back to the night I arrived at the wolf pack and the girl, Alena, lying in the back of a truck. She'd been beaten to a pulp, by vampires Calin suspected. He also felt they had a witch on their side, who had stopped her from transforming and prevented her from healing, using a potion or curse. I don't know about the healing, but it's my choice not to shift right now.

"I do heal faster," I tell him. "But only properly when I'm a wolf. Perhaps it's slowed down when I'm human because I haven't been transforming much lately and not for long when I do. Maybe that's what's going on."

"Well then, you need to transform. Go for a run."

"It's not that simple."

"Why not? You've got an entire forest here. How long do you think it would take? An hour? Two?"

I hadn't expected this from him, but the idea quickly takes root. The more I think about it, the more certain I am that the wolf part of me is adding to the pain. It needs letting out. So much for me thinking I was in control.

"What about the risk of being seen?"

"There's no one around, and I can keep a watchful eye out." He pauses. "By the way, when we arrived, I was told there are wolves in these parts."

"You never said."

"You never mentioned wanting to transform."

Werewolves are a lot bigger than run-of-the-mill ones. They shouldn't be of any concern to me, I reason.

"I don't know how long I'll need," I say, eventually.

After my fight with Daniel, it took a good few hours of walking, then gradually picking up the pace, to repair the damage he'd done.

"That's not a problem. I'll look after your clothes while you're gone."

"My clothes?"

"Well, you don't keep them on when you transform, do you?"

This is probably one of the strangest offers I've ever had, and yet for some reason, it makes me smile more than I've done in quite a while.

"That would be great," I say.

18

As I change to the wolf, the whimpering subsides. My muscles and bones stretch and break then click back into place in a manner that's way more satisfying than I'd ever thought possible. I stand there for a moment, absorbing the smells and sounds I'm now aware of. The air is sweet with the aroma of evergreen trees, the needles and pinecones. The earth smells richer here than it did in the forest of the pack. And I can hear insects scuttling in the undergrowth. I begin to move.

I haven't run once since my escape from Scotland, not even for a short burst. But now I'm here, feeling the cool wind blowing through my fur, it's all I want to do. I start with a slow trot, not much more than a walk really, then let myself go gradually faster until I'm almost flying through the trees.

Footpaths cross the forest and the scent of humans is quite strong in places, so I avoid them as best I can, keeping

CHAPTER 18

to the thickest and most dense areas, where the aroma of animals and plant life dominates. Gradually, the smell of the town and people fades and nature is all that's left.

Exhilarating as I find running again, the silence is almost unbearable, the emptiness in my head. It feels like it's been hollowed out and I've lost a vital part of me. A deep ache fills my chest, which has nothing to do with what I did last night. I find my thoughts drifting back to the pack. Not just Freya and Lou, but everyone, who I could have called family had I only given them the chance.

A glimmer of hope flickers within me. What if there aren't just ordinary wolves here? There must be other werewolf packs, surely? People like me. Concentrating my efforts, I try to pick up any hint of canine scent. After a few minutes, I do detect something in the undergrowth, but it's very weak—whoever or whatever it was, has not passed through here in quite a while. Still, I follow it as best I can, at the same time throwing out my thoughts like a net.

Hello! Is there anyone there? Hello! My name is Narissa. Can you hear me?

Each scent trail eventually leads to a dead end. It's only when I come up empty-handed for the fourth time that I finally remember Oliver. How long have I been gone? Certainly, more than an hour. The forest is so dense, I can't get a decent view of the sky, let alone the sun, to help me estimate the time of day. Slowing to a walk, I'm about to turn back, when something catches my eye a short way off. A clearing. It's so reminiscent of the one near the wolf village in Scotland, I have to investigate.

As I approach, my heart is pounding. What if I have found another pack? How would that work? My mother said that all wolves protect one another, (when they're not fighting for dominance, that is), but would that have only applied to the two packs she knew? How would I introduce myself, if I ever came across other werewolves?

I step into the open space and my heart sinks. There's no chance that wolves live here, unless they're nothing like I've experienced. There's a huge building, or rather the shell of one, surrounded by the remains of an old perimeter wall. A rusty iron gate marks the front of what must have once been the grounds of a magnificent manor house. More than half the roof has fallen in, and you can't see the brickwork at all in places for all the creepers that have taken over. You'd be risking life and limb if you ventured inside. No, nothing lives here, except maybe a few bats. In fact, the whole place gives off a distinct smell of death, the stench causing me to let out a low, involuntary growl.

Deciding that this is a sign to call it quits, I begin the long run back to Oliver. As I'm definitely on the road to recovery—and just for the hell of it—I decide to see how fast I can go.

"I TAKE IT YOU'RE FEELING BETTER," HE SAYS, AS WE MAKE our way home. "You're certainly not whinging so much."

"Honestly, it's like magic. Well, I guess it sort of is. Everything feels back to normal. If you could find a way to bottle this, you'd make a fortune."

"Well, I'm very pleased for you. And how was the run itself? Did you come across anything interesting?"

"Not really, just an old, derelict house. Other than that, just trees and more trees."

"It wouldn't be eastern Europe, would it, if there weren't some creepy, abandoned places about. Anyway, I was thinking, as we've got yesterday's earnings and you must be starving after such a long run, how about lunch at one of the restaurants by the river?"

"Really, isn't that a bit extravagant? Aren't we meant to be watching every penny, never mind lying low?"

"Well, now you mention it, you're right. Back for sandwiches, it is! What was I thinking?"

"No!" I grab his arm and pull him around. "I want nice food! You can't take it back now!"

We laugh together, then his smile drops.

"What is it?" I say, still holding onto his arm. "What's wrong?"

His eyes meet mine and there's the slightest of frowns on his face.

"Nothing. That's what is so strange. Right now, nothing feels wrong at all."

I gently release his arm.

"Actually, I think I've changed my mind. Let's just go for an ice-cream, instead."

After we've eaten our cones, chatting by the river, I realise it was nowhere near filling enough, and we decide to do some shopping before we go home. It's a really annoying cliché about the wolf, but it's definitely a carnivore. Meaning I'm also definitely a carnivore. Once, I could have happily lived on bread and cheese, but now only a juicy steak or roast chicken is going to do it for me.

How much life and our relationship has changed in these past few weeks. As Oliver said down by the water, if you ignore the fact that I've probably got the Vampire Council's best men trying to hunt me down and kill me and that I have no idea when I'll be able to return to my mother's pack, our day-to-day existence is pretty good. Simple, but good. Considering there was a time when I didn't think he and I would ever get back to talking civilly, at least one good thing has come out of all this crap.

We reach the butchers, and I notice that the bar we came to on our first night here, where Oliver sorted out a place for us to stay, is just across the way.

As we go to enter the shop, a man comes out of the bar waving his hands at us and calling something out.

"You go and buy what you want," Oliver says. "I'll deal with this."

"Do you think it's trouble?"

"No, I'm sure it isn't. He probably just wants to up the rent."

Leaving him to deal with whatever it is, I pick out some sausages and steaks. Back outside again, there's no sign of him. I guess whatever negotiations are taking place with our landlord, they may not be going well. Deciding he might need some moral support, I head over to the bar.

None of the light from outside seems to make its way to the interior, which is lit only by a couple of low-hanging lamps with nicotine-stained shades. A couple are sitting talking at the bar, and there are some tables dotted around, none of which are occupied. Blinking, I look around for Oliver, wondering where he can be. Then I spot a door at the back. As I walk towards it, it swings open.

"Narissa, what are you doing in here?"

"What do you mean? I came to meet you."

"Why didn't you wait outside? Like you were supposed to."

I don't like the tone of his voice and immediately feel my hackles rising.

"Supposed to? I'm sorry, I didn't realise I was on a leash. What's going on?"

"Nothing's going on. I'm fed up with you not listening to me, that's all."

And just like that, we're back to square one.

19

It would help if I could understand what just happened. One minute I'm basking in the warm glow of our relationship being back to normal, or as normal as possible in the current circumstances, and the next, Oliver won't even look me in the eye.

He shuns my offer to help cook dinner, which to be fair he'd do normally but in a jokey *you can't cook* way. Now, it's more like he can't stand to have me close to him. When the meal's ready, he dumps the plates on the table, sits down and starts digging into his without so much as a word.

Enough is enough. I may have put up with it before, but I will not let him do this to me again, when I've done nothing to deserve it. I'm certainly not going to let him blow hot and cold like this with no explanation. I figure whatever's wrong, I deserve better than that from our friendship.

"Just spit it out," I say, pulling out the chair opposite

him and sitting down. "What on earth is eating you? You were fine this afternoon."

"Nothing. It's just been a long couple of days, okay. I'm tired. Not everything is about you."

"So, I'm making too much of the fact that you won't even look at me. Is that it?"

He glances up from his food.

"I'm looking at you now, aren't I?" he says, and stares at me with a venomous glower.

Great. Truly reassuring.

"Oliver, I thought things were better between us. I thought …"

"You thought you'd got me back where you want me, acting as your dogsbody."

"What! That's not fair."

"Is it not?"

He stabs his fork into a piece of meat.

"Tell me," he demands. "Why does that vampire think about nothing but you."

"Polidori? You know why. Because of what I did to Styx."

"Not him. The other one. Sheridan."

My heart starts thumping.

"Calin? You've heard from him? What did he say? Did he have any news about my mother?"

"I haven't heard from him."

"Then—"

"I want to know why he's so obsessed with you, that's all."

This just isn't sitting right. He must have spoken to him.

"He's not obsessed. He just helped me."

"He hired a private helicopter for you. He killed a load of vampires for you. That's more than just helping."

"What do you want me to say?"

"The truth? How about that? Let's start with, are you in love with him?"

"What?"

"You heard me. Are you in love with him?"

This stuns me. Love is not an emotion I've ever experienced first-hand. Not in a romantic sense. It's something that other people naively chase. A delusion. What Calin and I felt for each other wasn't, couldn't be that.

"N—no ..." I stutter.

"You don't sound convinced."

"It's just—"

"It's just an easy question, or at least I thought it would be."

His tone is spiteful. Even with all that's gone wrong in the past, there was only one other time he's spoken to me like this. When he said he wanted me out of his life, forever.

"Where's all this coming from? I thought we were good."

"Because I want to know where I stand."

"Where you stand?"

"I mean, am I just babysitting you until you can run back into his arms—or his bed? You are screwing him, I presume?"

"What the hell?" I push myself away from the table with such force, my chair tips over. "How dare you?"

"I'm sorry, I thought we had a policy of honesty these days."

"Yeah, well, that's when I thought we were friends. I was obviously wrong there."

20

Oliver

I don't know why I let myself become so furious. I hate who I am when that happens. Anger isn't something I do, or rather wasn't, until we lost Rey. No. It was before that. It started when they forced her out of Blackwatch because of my stupid mistake. I flare up so easily, particularly at Naz. That girl has gone through so much, and I pile even more crap on her. How big an arsehole is it possible to be? Having this bloody vampire breathing down my neck all the time is sending me crazy.

It's the way he's insinuated himself into my life—into our lives—that riles me. But it's also the way he speaks to me, particular about her.

Today had been a good day. A really good day. For Naz,

even more than for me. I'd never say it to her face—for fear she'd rip me to shreds, literally—but I think she needs to let the wolf into her life more. Don't get me wrong, the fact my best friend is a werewolf scares the shit out of me, but that doesn't change who she is and what she needs. And she needs this wolf.

Whether she realises I know or not, I see the difference in her performance after she's taken herself off for five minutes during training. *Nature calls?* Honestly. I wish she would just be open about it, but then I guess transforming like that must be a pretty personal thing. Which is why today was such a breakthrough. Acknowledging what she needed. Letting me be a part of it—if looking after her clothes qualifies as that. She went running as a wolf for the first time since she left the pack. She let herself go, and when she returned, she was so calm, so relaxed. It was like the old Naz was back.

Then walking with her down by the river, I stupidly let my mind wander. Let myself daydream: we weren't on the run; her life wasn't in danger; I wasn't merely there as a glorified chaperone. We could have been any normal pair of friends, enjoying a city break together, eating ice creams and laughing. It was all so easy to imagine. And then we get back to town and I find he's left a message at the bar, telling me to contact him immediately. Like I'm at his beck and call.

Maybe it's down to my Blackwatch training, always obeying orders without a moment's hesitation. Or perhaps it's the fact that he's a member of the mighty Vampire

Council, but either way, I did as he requested. I didn't even wait until we got home and dig out the hidden mobile from the bottom of my bag. Instead, I used the payphone at the bar and called the number he'd left with the owner. God, how I wish I hadn't.

"Where've you been? I've been trying to contact you for hours."

"Why are you ringing me here?"

"Your phone's been switched off, going straight to answerphone every time."

"Yes, because I've been with Naz. We've been training."

"Okay, but you shouldn't stay out of contact for that long again. And you can't let her go running as a wolf either," he adds. "It would be too risky."

Jesus Christ. I immediately want to ring his neck.

"You are joking, right? Last time we spoke, you were worried that she wasn't changing enough."

"I wasn't fully cognisant of the situation then. They might be able to sense her if she transforms."

"They? Who?"

"The wolves."

"What wolves?"

"Don't worry. I'll take care of it."

As usual, he's only giving me half the story. I used to think that vampires were reticent because they needed to hide their secrets. Now I'm thinking, if they're all as arrogant as him, they can't have any friends to hang out with to practise normal conversation on.

"How's the training going?"

"Really well. She won three contests last night at a local fight club. She wants to go again in a week."

"What are you playing at? You're drawing attention to yourselves!"

"We need the money."

"I'll send you some!"

"We don't want it. Besides, it's good for Naz to have a purpose, and she needs real experience, more than I can ever give her. If you can't sort things out at your end, then it'll be even more crucial that she's able to defend herself."

"I guess I'll have to trust you."

I can't decide if that's a compliment or an insult, but there's no time to dwell on this before he's dishing out more orders.

"I have to go now," he says, like his time is infinitely more precious than mine. "Just make sure she doesn't transform. No runs. Nothing like that."

It's a miracle the handset doesn't crack, I'm gripping it that hard. The smile she had on her face when she came back from the forest this afternoon. Honestly, he has no idea what he's asking of me.

"Just so I get this straight. You want me to carry on hiding from her the fact that her mother is dead, most likely killed by her father's best friend. Keep her shut away, out of sight. And now deny her the one thing she has left to enjoy. Does that pretty much cover it?"

"I thought you told me you could handle this."

"I said I could keep her safe. What I can't handle is the constant change of rules. And she's forever asking about you, whether you've been in touch with any information about her mother. She's not an easy person to lie to."

There's a silence from his end of the line. I wish I could work out what he's thinking. I'm fairly sure, whatever it is, I'm not going to like it.

"Look, let me finish working out what's going on here. When I know for sure what we're up against, I'll come for her. Then you'll be free to go back to whatever it is you do."

"That's not what I meant."

"I really do have to go now. Stay in touch and keep me updated."

The line goes dead and I hang up the phone.

When I turn around and step back into the bar, Naz is just outside the door, looking straight at me. My stomach plummets and my blood runs cold. How long has she been there? My mind goes into overdrive, wondering how I'm going to lie my way out of this one. But I see the smile on her face and realise she couldn't have heard anything I said.

And then something snaps, and my anger and frustration pour out on her.

21

Narissa

He's an arsehole. A self-centred, arrogant arsehole.

Right now, I'm tempted to change and rip his fucking arm off. Seriously? I can take him resenting that he's giving up his life for me. I can take him blaming me for what happened to Rey. I deserve that. But to start questioning my sex life? Who does he think is he? My father?

I march into my room and slam the door then pick up my pillow, shove it against my face and scream. My fingernails are digging into the old fabric with such force that it starts to tear and I throw it on the bed. I've already learned that ripping up anything stuffed with feathers isn't such a good idea and I don't somehow think that Oliver would be quite so helpful with the cleaning up as Calin was.

I am so pissed off right now. He doesn't know the guy. He wouldn't even want to. So what, if I was screwing him? I've taken some far more dubious guys home in the past, even if they did have a pulse and a body registering more than room temperature. What's more, I'm bloody hungry and there's a perfectly good plate of food going cold out there on the kitchen table.

For the next hour, I distract myself with reading, or at least try to. I'm really only flicking through the pages while stewing about the situation. Finally, my stomach rumbling gets too much to bear. Putting my book down on the bed, I open my door a crack and see the one to Oliver's room is open, but there's no sign of him there or on the sofa, either. Great. So I'm now under lock and key, but he's free to come and go as he pleases. Flaming typical.

I walk through to the kitchen. Flicking on the light, I see a scrap of paper stuck to the fridge.

Sorry.

Dinner is in the oven.

O x

I'd like to be childish and leave it there, pretend I haven't seen it, not even left my room. But hunger overcomes my pettiness. I can't even wait to heat it up again. Cold steak is better than no steak at all.

"Time to get up."

CHAPTER 21

The sudden glare of light as Oliver opens my curtains causes me to duck my head under the covers.

"You're not serious?"

"Why wouldn't I be?"

After last night, the last thing I'd expected was a normal morning routine as if nothing had happened, and yet it's just gone daybreak and he's standing over me with toast and a cup of tea. I guess, combined with the note, this is his way of apologising, without actually verbalising the sentiment.

"I assume you want to keep up the training?" he says, putting the plate down on the bedside table. "If you don't, I understand."

He looks as guilty as hell and if I had an ounce more compassion in me, I'd say something to make him feel better. But a brief message and breakfast in bed aren't going to cut it. Still, I pick up the toast and take a bite.

"I probably need to shower first."

"I wouldn't bother. You're going to need one later, trust me."

On the positive side, I'm definitely getting fitter. The run today left me only moderately worn out, which is an improvement on a week ago. On the negative side, there's a small chance Oliver is, in fact, related to Satan.

"Push-ups, pull-ups, then burpees. Thirty reps of each. Six sets. Go."

"You know I can barely manage one pull up and my hands slip on that ruddy branch."

"Then you need to get practising."

He watches over me the entire time, chewing on his bottom lip, and only communicating when he yells at me for pausing to catch my breath. I'm on the last set of burpees, which at this point consist of me flopping down on the ground and then dragging myself back up, when he talks again.

"I spoke to Calin yesterday."

"What?" I can't have heard him right. Clearly, all this exertion has left me lightheaded.

"I spoke to Calin yesterday," he says, confirming I was right the first time. I get to my feet, my blood really pumping now.

"When? Why didn't you tell me?"

"Because he told me not to. He always tells me not to."

It takes a moment for the penny to drop.

"You mean you've talked with him before? What did he say? Did he tell you where Freya is? Did you ask him about her?"

As I move towards him, he shifts backwards, his hands out in front of him, like there's the chance I could suddenly lunge at him, which I might.

"He hasn't told me anything about her, Naz."

"Have you asked him?"

"Of course, I have. I ask him plenty of questions and

he doesn't answer any of them, ever. I don't know where he is or what he's doing. He rings occasionally to check on you and then hangs up."

"And you didn't think I deserved to know this?"

"I did. I wanted to tell you, but he swore me to secrecy."

My last nerve frays.

"Swore you to secrecy? Are you five years old? You should have let me talk to him. You should have let me ask him about Freya."

"I understand. But there are bigger things at play here, Naz. Things involving the Council. And Blackwatch."

"So, he's told you that much."

"Only in a roundabout way. Please, Naz."

He stretches out a hand towards me, only to withdraw it at my snarl. Taking a deep breath, he steps back again, hands up in front of himself once more.

"Look, I do understand how you might think I've been wrong on this. But the guy got you away safely. He got you out of a vampire dungeon, too. I figured if he said to keep you out of the loop, it was the right thing to do."

My fists are balled at my sides. How I haven't thrown him against the nearest tree is a goddamn miracle. I somehow manage to keep myself in check.

"So, why are you telling me all this now? Why not just stay quiet?"

He takes another deep breath, which tells me I'm not going to like what he says next, either. Gritting my teeth, I steel myself.

"He said you shouldn't be running about as a wolf. He said it was dangerous."

"What? Why?"

"I don't know. Naz, he doesn't explain *anything*. I think maybe he's worried about other wolves. But I'm just guessing."

"There are no other wolves," I snap back. "I would have felt them if there were."

He nods, his eyes still locked on mine.

"It's not me trying to stop you, Naz. I had to be straight with you where the order was coming from. I couldn't keep it to myself any longer and I thought you had a right to know. I'm sorry."

God, what a fucking shit show this has become. Two years ago, the worst thing we had to apologise to each other for was finishing off the milk or eating the last slice of pizza. Now we're struggling to get through one week without some massive bust up.

"It was just sex," I blurt out, before stopping to think.

This time is Oliver's turn to do a double take.

"Calin and I. You were right. We are …we were … but it was just a distraction. That's all."

"A distraction?" He snorts, and for a second, I want to lash out at him, but then I see all the hurt in his eyes. Hurt and disbelief.

"It was at the wolf pack. The first—the only—time. There was stuff going on with Freya and I just needed … I just needed …"

CHAPTER 21

"A distraction," he says, throwing my words back at me, then shaking his head. "Oh, Naz, I wish you could see it."

"What?"

"You are worth so much more than a distraction."

He steps close to me for the first time since we started this row, and I can see a hundred different thoughts whirring behind his eyes. That's always been Oliver's way. Always thinking. Weighing up the pros and cons, the positives and negatives. I guess that served him well at Blackwatch but it's handicapped him in real life.

As we stand there in the forest, I feel myself being drawn slowly towards him. It was Oliver I wanted to see one last time when I thought my life was about to end. He was the one I so desperately needed to speak to.

I want him to know how much he means to me. I should tell him that now.

Just as I'm about to, he straightens up and plasters a fake smile on his face.

"So, are we going to do some fighting today or not?"

22

I have no idea where this last week has gone. No, that's not true, it's been spent almost entirely on training in preparation for tonight.

Bizarrely, since I confessed to Oliver about sleeping with Calin, our relationship has improved. I wasn't aware of it at the time, but keeping it to myself was like a massive weight bearing down on me. Now that it's been removed, I can breathe easier. I think that Oliver admitting to his secret conversations with Calin has had the same effect on him.

I'm still moderately pissed off, mind you, mainly that he didn't ask for more details about my mother and the wolf pack, but it's understandable. To him, Calin is a member of the big, bad Vampire Council. A killer. I'm not surprised he didn't want to push things. I, on the other hand, have no intention of sticking to the rules. Particularly the one about not changing into a wolf.

Whether it's stubbornness or spite, I've been for a run every day since he told me about Calin's order not to, and I've at last got used to the silence in my head. I stick to the same route: a large lap of the forest—skirting the freaky abandoned house that smells of death—then alongside a brook, until I hit the main path back to where Oliver sits reading a book, guarding my clothes.

While I keep my mental blocks in place, it hasn't stopped me sending out my thoughts in search of any other werewolves that might be nearby. But there's never any reply and all I can detect is the smell of the wild, natural, non-shifting wolves.

Oliver has promised me faithfully that the next time Calin rings, he'll let me speak to him, but he also says he doesn't know when that will be. And I do believe him. Fortunately, I have enough to distract myself with.

WE ARRIVE LATE. HE SAID IT WOULD BE A GOOD TACTIC TO help unnerve my opponents and increase the betting odds. I don't know if he's right. This time, eyes are on both of us as we make our way through the arena. Some people don't seem particularly pleased to see us. I'm looking more the part tonight, wearing a suitable outfit, the jeans and baggy T-shirt abandoned. I can't say I feel comfortable in the short-cropped top and equally short shorts, but I will admit it looks like I belong here and mean business.

As I approach, the girl with the braids rolls her eyes.

"I'm not fighting that one," she says to the man next to her. "She's a nutter."

I lock eyes with her, a smirk on my face, hoping to provoke her into fighting me again.

"So, who shall we start with?" I ask. "Someone tough. I want a good fight."

Maybe I'm being naïve, but I'm feeling so much stronger that I'd like to begin the first bout without relying on the wolf to come to my aid. I'll obviously call on it when I need to.

Two men are currently rolling around on the mat inside the cage. Both broad, both bald. It's hard to tell who's winning from the tumbling flesh. I watch them for a minute before Oliver taps my arm. One of the organisers is waving at him, trying to get his attention.

"I guess they've got someone lined up for you," he says.

***

The winner stumbles from the cage and the loser is carried out as we await my turn to fight. I sense movement behind me and turn to see the crowd separating as my opponent swaggers towards me.

"Oliver, there's no way I can fight that girl. She looks barely eighteen."

"Then it'll be fast. This isn't on you. She signed up for this. And they saw you fight last time, so they know what they're doing. Just don't go too hard. End it cleanly and quickly. No over-indulging the wolf."

"When do I ever do that?"

He raises an eyebrow.

"Okay, I've got it. Clean and quick."

Not wanting to waste time overthinking it, I step through the cage door. When she joins me, my concern increases. I'd assumed that the long, loose hair and all the necklaces and bracelets were simply for effect as she approached the ring, but her hair remains down and she's still sporting all her jewellery. There's no way she can have any experience at all. A baggy T-shirt was nearly the end of me in my first fight. With no rules to adhere to, there's nothing to stop me from grabbing one of those chains and dragging her to the floor with it. The commitment she's shown to her eyeliner, on the other hand, is more than I'd bother with on a night out—although I'm not sure if that says more about her or me.

"Thank you," she says, finally drawing her hair up into a high ponytail.

"For what?" I ask, a little confused.

"For giving me the opportunity to kick your arse."

Clearly, she's not the brightest light in the harbour. Now I feel even more guilty that I'm about to spoil her makeup.

Outside the ring a far larger crowd is drawing close than for my previous fights. Perhaps news of me has spread.

The ref steps into the cage and indicates for us to take our places. A bell rings and it's time to fight.

23

The clang is still ringing in my ears as she darts towards me and lands a hard right hook into my ribs. Winded, I jump back and catch my breath. I wasn't prepared for that. Fortunately, she doesn't follow it up.

I shake my head and click my neck before moving back to the centre of the ring jabbing at her once, then again. Both times, she dodges skilfully.

"What a shame," she says, her feet motionless as I bounce around on my toes the way Oliver taught me. "I'd thought this would be more fun. Don't worry. I'll end it fast."

She fires out a leg this time, sweeping my feet from under me and sending me crashing face down to the cold, blood-stained canvas. I lie there, startled and winded.

"Get up Naz!" I hear Oliver yell. "You know what to do. Get up and fight. You can do this."

I scramble to my feet, surprised she didn't jump on me.

CHAPTER 23

When I turn to face her, she's standing there, grinning. She's playing with me.

I go on the attack again, and again she slips past my punch, countering with a fist to my temple. I stagger back. This time she does carry on. Fast, stinging blows rain down on my arms as I raise them to protect myself. I kick out at her, but she casually sweeps my leg aside, spinning me around. I need the wolf, but for some reason, it's not showing up. Perhaps all those long runs I've been taking to spite Calin, have had the wrong effect. Maybe the only reason it was so keen to join in before was because it wanted some action and now it doesn't feel the need to show up. Shit. Why didn't I think of that? How the hell am I going to get out of this in one piece now?

She slams my face into the bars and starts landing punches in my kidneys. With all the strength I can summon, I push myself away from the cage and spin away to face her. But before I can orientate myself, her foot slams into my stomach and I'm back on the bars again. The metal is cold against my bare flesh. Whatever's coming next, I know it's going to hurt.

The crowd is going wild. I search fleetingly for Oliver before my attention returns to my opponent in time to see her gleeful smile and her fist flying through the air. It lands squarely on my jaw. Everything flashes white. My legs buckle, and I know I'm going to collapse but find myself held upright by her forearm across my windpipe. I can feel myself slipping into unconsciousness. I need the wolf!

Come on! I scream inside my head. *Where are you? What the hell are you playing at?*

I feel a growl reverberate in my skull.

Please! I need you!

"You want more?" the girl asks with a grin. "I can oblige."

Her eyes narrow as she moves her arm back to take another punch. Bracing myself, I take a deep breath and squeeze my eyes shut for a millisecond. I feel the disturbance in the air as her hand flies towards me, and then, like it's the most natural thing in the world, I catch her wrist, her fist barely an inch from my nose.

It's like waking from a deep sleep. Finally, I feel alive again. It's me and the wolf, together.

Her eyes widen as I tighten my grip. I use my other hand to prise her arm from my throat and twist it back. I feel her muscles weaken. She's obviously no pushover, but her technique is actually rather sloppy.

"At last," I say with a smirk. "Now I'm ready for a fight."

I bring my forehead down hard on the bridge of her nose, then release her. She staggers backwards and I slam my foot into her exposed midriff. As she doubles over, I aim a solid right hook at her temple. There's far more force behind the blow than I've ever managed before. She goes down on one knee and puts a hand on the mat to steady herself. I wait for the ref to step in, but he doesn't.

The girl slowly raises her head and looks at me. My blood runs cold. Where have I seen that expression before?

"I like this," she says.

Before I realise what's happening, she's on her feet and has launched herself at me. I twist away, escaping her fist, but it's so close, I feel the rush of air at the side of my face. I move to a better position, but she's already set to go. *How on earth?*

I barely have time to catch another breath before her leg flies around again and catches me. I land awkwardly on my back. She's straight on me this time and there's no escaping her punches as they find their mark once, twice and then a third time, knocking my head from side to side. How is she managing this? The wolf is there, fighting back too. I can feel it. And yet her strength is a match for mine.

The crowd is on its feet baying for blood, although whose, I couldn't say.

"Get up, Naz. Fight back!"

That voice. I remember when I thought Daniel was about to end my life and all I wanted was one last chance to tell Oliver how I felt about him.

The girl is looming over me, fists raised.

That's all she is, I remind myself, *just a girl and I am so much more than that. I've taken down vampires, and there's no way I'm letting her beat me.*

Catching her hands, I throw her to the left and we roll across the canvas in a jumble of limbs. I free myself and flick back onto my feet. It turns out all those drills are paying off.

She's relied entirely on strength and quick reflexes, I think, as she too jumps up.

I clear my mind and let the wolf take control.

I dodge from side to side to avoid her fists. I must play to her weakness, which is her technique. I need to get her into a position where she has no way out. And that's exactly what I do.

I don't let up for a second. Every time I land a punch, I'm already firing off the next. Noticing she's off-balance, I sweep at her legs. She falls awkwardly, and I bring my elbow down on her shoulder before she can get up. I go to follow with a kick, but she's on the move again. This time, though, the wolf knows exactly what she will do. I spin, bringing as much momentum to my right arm as I can. She stands just in time for me to connect cleanly with her jaw and she drops to the ground, stunned. The ref lifts my hand.

The arena erupts with applause and whistles. They're cheering for me! I turn to the four sides of the cage and pump the air with my fists.

As I make my way to the door, my eyes move across the crowd, searching for Oliver. When I finally locate him, I freeze. He's not smiling. He's not even looking at me. He's looking past me. He seems horror-struck. His eyes are almost bulging.

24

The crowd is still going wild. I turn around. The girl is up off the canvas. Her top lip folds back in a snarl, and that's when I see them—two gleaming fangs. Oliver yanks the cage door open and pulls me out. The vampire moves to follow me. I lose sight of her as Oliver and I are encircled by fans. It doesn't take us long to untangle ourselves, but by the time we do, she's disappeared.

"Where did she go?" I ask.

"I didn't see, Naz. I'm so sorry. I had no idea there were vampires here."

"That doesn't matter now. We have to find her, stop her before she can tell anyone about me."

He turns around. "There's only one way in or out of here. The staircase. She must have gone that way."

I don't wait for him to say more. I race through the crowd, scattering people as I go. Reaching the staircase, I take the steps two, then three, at a time. I don't know how

I'm managing it I'm so exhausted. I have to catch up with her. Yet even as I'm saying this to myself, I feel it's an impossible task. She has too much of a lead on me, and as soon as she's outside, she'll be off in a flash. With the last of the adrenaline, I push through the door and step out into the night. My stomach sinks.

Oliver emerges just moments after me.

"We've lost her," he pants, looking around. "She could have gone anywhere. We'll never track her down."

"*You* can't," I reply, and without further ado, I start pulling off my clothes.

"No, Naz, you mustn't. People might see."

"We've no other choice," I say, throwing him my things. "She mustn't get away."

A second later, the wolf springs forwards.

I can smell her immediately, that deathly aroma weaving its path through those of the living. I race between the metal containers, the cold concrete hard under my paws compared to the grass I'm used to. I turn a corner, then the next, and then … nothing. The scent has disappeared, just like that. I stop and look around. Then up. That's the only place she could have gone.

I've jumped many things as a wolf but all at ground level. Height has never come into it. Until now.

Moving back a few yards to give myself a run up, I leap into the air for all I'm worth. My front paws land on the roof of the top container. Nails scrabbling on the rusty metal, my back ones join them. I'm on the scent again, chasing her under the moonlit sky.

CHAPTER 24

It becomes a dance of twists and turns, ups and downs. The vampire girl is trying to confuse me. No doubt she can hear me racing behind her. I'm well and truly latched onto her now, and I'm closing in. But do I continue as a wolf and simply kill her? It's tempting but then what? I won't get the answers I need. Why was she there tonight? Was it because someone else told her? Could Polidori have sent her? I have to know.

One more turn between the containers, and I'll have her, and I know exactly what I'm about to come face-to-face with. Whether it's sensible or not, I transform back to human and step around the corner.

In this light, she looks even more immature, definitely younger than me but possibly even Lou, too.

"What are you?" she asks, her eyes wide. "I thought you were like us, but you're not, are you?"

I step forwards, confused. Whatever I was expecting, it wasn't that.

"Who knows I'm here?" I ask, trying to look as intimidating as I can given that I'm completely starkers. "Does Polidori? Have you spoken to him?"

She takes a step towards me. We're now only an arm's length from each other. She reaches out her hand, and for a second, I think she's going for my neck. Instead, she takes a strand of my hair in her fingers, brings it to her nose and sniffs deeply.

"You're different. I've never smelled anything like you before. Are you part of it, too?"

I'm still torn between ripping her throat out and

quizzing her for answers. Something about her is so *off*. She's definitely a vampire; there was no mistaking the teeth or the smell once I'd locked onto it, but this behaviour is downright odd.

"You're not like the others they bring," she says, "Are you joining us? Are you part of it, too?"

Again, that question.

"I'm not joining you for anything."

Her face falls, like a toddler who's just been told they can't have ice cream for breakfast.

"So, you're not part of the uprising?" she demands, her expression changing to something altogether fiercer. "You should be with us. It's the right thing to do. It's what we deserve, our rightful place."

She snarls, eyes flickering darkly as she exposes her fangs. *Both* sets of fangs: top *and* bottom. My stomach lurches. She may not be one of Polidori's people, but she's something equally dangerous.

Then, just as quicky, her demeanour switches again. Fear flashes in those unblinking eyes.

"Are you going to tell them?"

"Tell who?"

"The others. They don't know I came. We're not meant to leave. Not supposed to feed yet. But I didn't, did I? So they can't be cross. You won't tell them, will you?"

My confusion is growing by the second. There are no two ways about it—she's a vampire, obviously a rogue, with intact bottom fangs like that. But the way she's looking at me. The terror in her expression. I remember what Calin said about vampires turning people as playthings, then discarding them without teaching them what they are or how to survive. This must be the case with her. But who does she mean by *the others?*

"Please." She's begging now. "Please. You're different too, like me, aren't you? I know you are."

God, my heart's hurting. How long ago was she human, I wonder? It can't have been very long, to not even be aware of what I am. But then she didn't lose control back in the ring, when I was bleeding. Which means she must be well fed. Everything about her is a contradiction. Well, almost everything. No matter what brought her here, there's only one way this can end.

"I'll make it swift," I say, the only comfort I can offer her … and transform.

25

"Oh Christ!" Oliver's first words when he finally joins me sum up the situation pretty succinctly.

I turn around, sweat running down my spine. Even in the shadows, there's no disguising the fact that I am once again butt naked, although that's not currently my biggest concern.

"Did you see what happened?"

From the way the blood has drained from his face, I can't help but think that's the case. It was bad enough doing it, but for him to witness that side of me—it's not something I ever wanted.

"I've just got here. Did she hurt you?"

His eyes go from me to the vampire's body, and then to her head, lying a few feet away.

"Shit, Naz. We'll have to get our stuff from the flat quickly and go."

I take my clothes from him and he averts his gaze as I get dressed.

I look down at the aftermath of my encounter and consider the situation. The fact that he didn't see me ruthlessly kill a deranged vampire kid calms my nerves a fraction, but it doesn't change the bizarreness of what just went down.

"She wasn't from the Council," I tell him. "She wasn't looking for me. She didn't even know what I was."

He frowns. "How can you be sure?"

"She told me. She spoke to me. She *wanted* to speak to me."

"But if she wasn't sent by the Council, then what?"

"She was a rogue—exactly how Calin described them—and had no real idea what she was. And she still had her bottom fangs."

"So, one of the Council members must have turned her. Someone out hunting for you got hungry and careless. This doesn't make the situation any better, Naz. We have to get going. Now."

He reaches out and takes my hand, but I don't move. I can't stop staring at her. It's like she's part of a giant jigsaw puzzle and I should be able to figure out how all the pieces fit together.

"It can't have been a member of the Council who turned her," I say. "That's impossible. None of them have their bottom fangs, except Polidori."

"Well, that means she must have been turned by another rogue, and even if there's only one more out there, that's still bad news, Naz. You've left your scent all over the place."

"So, she wasn't working for Polidori." I recap. "She wasn't even after me in particular. She definitely didn't know I was a werewolf, but she knew I was special. She knew she was special too, but not what she actually was. But she was fixated on whether I was going to join her."

"Join her?"

"As part of an uprising."

"What! Naz, that sounds bad. Really bad. We definitely can't hang around."

I know he's right but I need a minute longer to think.

"Oliver, if there's a rogue here, killing innocent girls like she must once have been, shouldn't I at least try to find it before we leave?"

"No. No, you absolutely should not."

"But I can kill it, Oliver, easily. I can kill a dozen of them if needs be."

"No, the answer is no. We go back to the flat for our gear, get back on the road and we don't stop until we're a thousand miles away."

My eyes return once more to the mutilated girl. He's right, but there's something about her that makes me particularly uneasy, and I can't put my finger on what it is.

"Fine, we'll leave," I say.

I know we need to go on the run again. Killing her may cause ripples that we can't predict. As we walk back through the containers, the silence between us extends.

We reach the gates of the yard. The river and town

come into view. I feel sad. This place wasn't home, not by a long shot, but it's the most time I've spent anywhere since I left London. I'm going to remember it for a many reasons. The padlocked bridge. Those floral curtains. The runs in the forest past the creepy old house.

And that's when it hits me.

26

"I have to go now. I need to know for sure."

"Naz, I don't like this. I don't like it at all."

"It'll be fine. By the time I get there, the sun will be coming up. Daylight hours. I just want to know if I'm right, if it's a nest."

I'm furious at myself for not realising sooner, but then again, why would I? When I first tackled vampires as a wolf, I was more concerned about not dying than taking note of what they smelled like. The only other vampire I've been near in wolf form is Calin and we were only together like that briefly, in Scotland. Once when I followed his scent through the forest back to the village and again when he ran with me to the cabin. I didn't think about the subtleties of his aroma then. He just smelled of Calin to me. But the scent of the girl—of decaying rottenness—is the same one that's caught my attention every time I've passed that house.

"Say it is a vampire nest, then what would you want to do, Naz?"

"What do you think I'd want to do? I'd want to destroy it. Kill them all. Stop them changing more innocent people!"

He drops his head into his hands and sighs, then lifts it again and looks at me.

"How about this? The next time I hear from Calin, I tell him to deal with it. That's part of his job, isn't it? Eliminating rogues. We leave today, move on to safety and he looks after things here."

"No." My answer is immediate. "He won't be able to come here at the drop of a hat. He's pretending to hunt me, remember, and it could be weeks before he gets in touch again. Besides, the last thing he'll want to do is draw attention to where we've been. And every night nothing is done, is an opportunity for those vampires to be out murdering."

A shadow crosses his face. I know he hates me talking about Calin.

"Please," I say. Just let me go for one more run to see if I'm right. Then, if I am, we'll figure out what our next course of action is. Together. Just a few hours are all I'm asking for, Oliver. Please."

"Fine, but meanwhile I'm packing our bags. I want to be ready to leave the moment you're back."

"Unless I'm right."

"We'll see."

I AM A HUNDRED PERCENT RIGHT. THE MOMENT I APPROACH the house, it's there. A stench like rotting wet leaves. Like putrefying flesh. It catches in the back of my throat. How did I not know about this before? And why didn't Calin smell this way to me? No wonder Lou and the others were so freaked out by him. I would have been too if I'd caught a whiff of it. I can't dwell on that right now. I've got to concentrate on staying safe.

My nerves are on edge as I step out of the forest and head towards the house. I'm sure I'll be all right. I've done plenty of runs around here before and they've never tried to follow me come night-time. This is different, though. I'm the one doing the hunting and my first task is to find out how many of these bloodsuckers there are.

There's no need to rush, I tell myself as I approach what's left of the wrought-iron gates and the crumbling brick wall that marks the boundary of the property. It's sunrise. If they're newly turned, they won't have built up any tolerance to daylight. Even Calin prefers to be fully covered. And anyway, there would need to be a lot of them if they wanted to take me down.

I circle once, then again, then a third time, trying to detect any sounds from within, but it's eerily silent. Outside, there's no birdsong, not even any insect noise. What kind of place has no creepy crawlies? I guess this type of place.

After my third lap, I feel I've got as good a measure of

the situation as I'm going to. It's hard to distinguish exactly between the aromas, but if I had to make an educated guess, I'd say there are somewhere between half a dozen and ten vampires inside. A dozen max. One scent is stronger than the others. It leads away from the house. It's the one I was chasing down only a couple of hours ago. Again, I feel a deep sadness for the young life I was forced to end. She had once been just a girl, a sweet one probably, too.

There's one other distinct smell outside, but it's not vampire, nor anything living. It's of exhaust and rubber tyres, still present on the grass and stones leading up to the gate. A car. Someone's been here and left again. A food delivery? Probably not of the pizza variety.

A yawn stretches my jaw, followed promptly by my stomach growling. Knowing I've uncovered as much information as I'm likely to, and confident this is an issue I can deal with later, I turn and leave.

I've just reached the edge of the forest again when I hear a soft humming noise. No, more a buzzing, but it's so gentle I wonder for a moment if I dreamt it. I concentrate. It was more a feeling than a sound and the sensation has already passed.

I freeze.

Hello? I send out. *Is someone there? Is there someone else here?*

I've done this a hundred times since I left the pack. Calling out into the ether, hoping for a reply and getting nothing. But this time, something feels different. My skin tingles and my hackles rise.

Is anyone there? I try again.

I wait, motionless, begging the feeling to return.

There it is! The impression of someone encroaching on the boundary of my block. I reach out again, desperate for confirmation. But I'm confused. Surely, I would have felt something before this? I could sense any of the wolves in the pack without being on high alert the whole time.

The minutes tick by as I stand there, stretching my mind out as far as I can, just as Art and Lou taught me. But I find nothing but emptiness. Nothing to connect with.

I run back into the forest, in case I can pick up a scent. But eventually I'm forced to give up. It's not the first time my senses have let me down recently. Not identifying the girl as a vampire with all that staring and lack of blinking is evidence of that. Still, I'm saddened. Another wolf could have been an ally in what I must do next.

Slowly, I retreat through the forest, keeping my mind as alert as I can. I'm struggling, though. Tiredness, I realise, probably led me to imagine things. I haven't stopped and rested since the fight last night. My body took such a pounding. I should be concentrating on healing. The best thing I can do now, is to go back to the flat and get a couple of hours' sleep, before I attempt to convince Oliver of my plan. Not that I actually have one yet. I've got to figure that part out, too.

27

Oliver

I don't blame myself for not telling Naz about Freya. Maybe that makes me a complete arsehole, but I can't be the one to tell her that her mother's dead, especially after she'd only just found out she was still alive. When she told me about it, there was no hiding the love in her eyes, despite all the hurt she'd originally felt. Then, a couple of days later, that damn vampire calls me to tell me she'd been murdered, and I've had to shoulder the weight of that bloody secret for months. Things have just started to get better between us. When she discovers what I've been hiding from her, the shit's going to hit the fan, to put it mildly.

The last few days, I've been going back and forth over

it, trying to work out if I've made the right call, and I'm still no closer to an answer. There's no going back on it now, no matter how guilty I feel. It's not even just a case of finding the right words. I won't be able to answer any of her questions. I wasn't there. She'll have all these things she'll immediately need to know, and I won't be able to say anything useful to help ease the pain.

Besides, and maybe this *is* shit of me, but why should it be down to me? I'm the one trying to keep everything together for her. That fucking vampire's the one who wanted to hide the truth from her in the first place. He's the one who ought to deal with the fallout. And not to be petty or anything, but he's the one who screwed her. Even with a pulse, he wouldn't be half the man she deserves. Although I'm starting to wonder if I'm any better.

Flicking on the kettle, I pace around the kitchen table, checking my watch for the tenth time in as many minutes. She should be back by now. I ought to have gone with her. Or better still, not let her go at all. This lying has got to me so much, I wasn't thinking straight. Trying to keep Naz safe against the combined efforts of Blackwatch and the Vampire Council, then seeing what she did last night, I'm so messed up in the head that I'm making stupid mistakes, and that's not like me.

Leaving the kettle to boil, I sink onto the sofa. I can't stop thinking about all the untruths that have spilled from my lips this last week. I want to come clean, but I just don't see how I can now. If I own up, not just about her mum, but about having a phone and being able to contact Calin, she'd be furious, seriously furious, and Naz doesn't act like the most rational person, even at the best of times. I know what would happen. The moment it came out, she'd head for the forest, turn into a wolf and disappear. Leaving me no way of finding or protecting her. It's a risk that I can't take. Won't take.

I close my eyes to see if that helps, but in less than half a minute, they snap open again. All the worst-case scenarios are running through my head simultaneously. If she finds a nest, then I know what comes next. She's going to want to get rid of it. From what I saw last night, she'd make swift work of that.

Once again, I shudder at the memory of what I saw her do. Whatever I'd imagined her abilities as a wolf were, it's clear I grossly underestimated them. She was ruthless. Yet there was compassion in the last words she spoke to the girl. When she turned and saw me there and asked if I'd seen what had happened, I knew what she wanted the answer to be. I knew she needed to keep that part of herself separate from me, and so I lied. Again.

The truth is, I'm terrified of pushing her away. I did it once before, after we lost Rey and I very nearly lost Naz for good then. Stuff was said in the heat of the moment; you always think there'll be a chance to take it back and make things right. But sometimes there's not.

Part of me feels like this a twisted form of karma. I got so mad at her for lying to me. I said some truly shitty things. At the time, I didn't see how it was possible to say you genuinely care for someone and keep so much from them. Now, I find out it's alarmingly easy; you've just got to convince yourself you're doing the right thing. But I'm done with all that. From this point on, I'll be as honest as I can. I'll worry about those previous lies later.

I'm about to get up to make coffee, when the door opens. She looks exhausted. There are deep shadows under her eyes and her hair is plastered to her face. Yet she still looks perfect to me. If I could, I'd wrap my arms around her and take her away from all this, forever. But that's not an option. She steps into the flat, closes the door behind her, then heads to the cupboard and pulls down two mugs.

"So, do you want the good news or the bad news?" she asks.

28

Narissa

I place the mugs on the counter, aware that I probably look a complete and utter wreck. The wolf may aid the healing process, but nothing can help with being covered in mud or being desperately tired, other than a long soak in the bath and a good sleep. I'm seriously in need of both. And by the looks of things, I'm not the only one.

Oliver is bleary-eyed, clearly not having rested either. Pushing himself up from the sofa, he shakes his head as if to clear it.

"Bad first," he says, finding his voice. "You should know that by now. If you start with the good news, I'd be too busy worrying about what the bad is. Is it really bad? Just tell me. Let's get it over with."

"Fair enough." I grab two tea bags from the caddy. "The bad news is that it definitely is a vampire nest."

"Shit. There's something good to follow that?"

"It's small. Ten vampires at most."

"Ten is small?"

"Well, I think so. And they don't seem to be leaving the house much."

He nods, and I pour water into the mugs, waiting for whatever's coming next.

"So, how are these ten agoraphobic vampires getting fed?"

"I think they're having blood delivered. I caught the scent of a car. I'm only guessing, but I'd say it was maybe a couple of days old. Definitely not fresh, though. From what Calin told me, they don't actually need to feed that often. Perhaps Blackwatch is supplying them or someone raided a local hospital."

I think of the fridges filled with bags of blood at the Blood Bank bar. How long would a supply like that keep ten vampires going? Although why they would stay in one place and not explore, is a whole other matter.

"So, what does that mean? What happens now?" Oliver asks, interrupting my thoughts.

What indeed.

I've spent the whole journey back trying to figure out the next bit. How do I convince him I can take them down? And not only that I can, but that I should. I know we're in hiding to protect my life, but this isn't just about me. What happens if I don't act? Whoever they are, the fact they probably all have their bottom fangs means they don't follow the Blood Pact. Sooner or later, they'll start leaving the nest, just like the girl did, and when that happens, they'll want to do more than go three rounds in a boxing ring. I'm not sure how I can say that to Oliver without him thinking I've got some kind of death wish.

"Now, I know you're going to get all up in arms about this," I start carefully. "But ten vampires are nothing to a werewolf. I can handle them."

"I believe you."

"You do?"

"And you want to take them out?"

"I do."

"Okay."

This is odd. I have a whole list of arguments prepared. The fact that I don't seem to need them makes me feel decidedly uneasy. He's treated me as a liability the entire time we've been on the run, and yes he's been training me, but that doesn't feel like a reason for his opinion to change so abruptly. Then it clicks into place.

"You saw me last night," I say, lowering myself onto one of the dining chairs. "You got there before I killed her, didn't you? But you said you hadn't when I asked you. Why?"

He dips his chin, avoiding eye contact for a moment before looking up again.

"I didn't know what to say. It seemed like you'd prefer me not to have been there."

"Of course, I would. Do you imagine I wanted you to watch me murder a young girl?"

"A vampire, Naz. And you did what you had to do. The way you did it was … was …" He pauses and I wait for whatever horrendous adjective he's going to come up with. "… merciful."

"But I killed her. I could have shown her more mercy and let her live."

"No, Naz, you couldn't. The poor girl was a lost soul. She was a danger to us and to all the people of this city, just like the rest of them are. I'll admit I'm not happy about you attacking a vampire nest single handed. In fact, the thought fills me with utter dread, but I get it, and I know I can't stop you. You need to do what you have to do. And if you're confident that you can achieve it, then I trust you."

Jesus Christ. Of all the things I wasn't expecting, it was the conversation to go like this. Maybe I should have let him see me rip a head off sooner, although it must make it difficult to view someone as a helpless damsel in distress when you get to see them as a 250 pound beast with two-inch canines.

I lift my mug and take a sip of tea, to give myself the chance to digest this massive turnaround.

"Okay. That's great. I'll deal with it."

I watch the tension ripple through him, but he manages to contain it, just.

"I assume you have a plan," he says. "And you know I'll be coming with you."

I slam my mug back down on the table, slopping tea everywhere.

"No way. It's too dangerous."

"No. If it's as safe as you say it is, then having me there won't be a problem. Besides, I do have experience with vampires."

"As a peacekeeper! You fill in spreadsheets and organise their blood supplies. Your job is to foster good relations between them and humans. This is not the same thing at all."

"It's non-negotiable, Naz," he says. "If anything were to happen to you—"

"No!"

His jaw locks and he glowers at me.

"Look, Naz, I will walk into that vampire nest myself if you make this difficult. I am not letting you do this on your own. So, either we work together on this or you're going to have a darn sight more to worry about."

Damn his stubbornness. I do love him for it, but right now, it makes me want to throttle him.

The air leaves my nose in a long hiss.

"I'm in charge." There's no hint of a question in my voice. "If you're joining me, you do everything I say. Particularly when I need you out of the way. I can't communicate to you as a wolf and if I have to turn back to human—well we saw how fighting one of them like that went last night."

"Okay, I agree. Whatever the plan is, I'll stick to it. I swear."

"Good."

I'm still not convinced it's a good idea, but if I can place him somewhere out of harm's way, maybe it'll work.

"So," he says, looking eager to appease me. "What's the plan?"

I take a sip of tea and then an enormous yawn escapes my lips.

"Maybe we could start with a quick nap."

29

Shit. This was definitely not part of the plan. A quick power nap was what I told Oliver I needed. Just an hour under my grotesque floral bedsheets and I'd be refreshed and ready to go. That was eight hours ago.

Being annoyed at myself is my normal state of mind, but this time I'm really pissed off.

"You should have woken me up," I spit at him.

"You were fast asleep. You needed the rest."

"What I needed was to attack that nest at midday. It's too late to go now." I pace the room, kicking the bottom of the sofa as I go. "It's getting dark now. I suppose if I leave straight away and run there—"

"No," he says quickly. Not that I need much convincing. Even I'm not really reckless enough to consider taking on a nest at night.

"Don't worry, I'm not going to do anything stupid. It has to be light when I attack."

"So, what do you have in mind?" he asks.

"It's more of a rough overview than a concrete, detailed play-by-play. But the more I think about it, the more convinced I am that it'll work. We need to get them outside," I say, talking through my thought process, "into the midday sun."

"And how do you plan on achieving this?"

"By setting fire to the house."

Oliver cocks his head and raises a brow. I expect him to disagree, but for the moment, he's not.

"I can see that could work. And then?"

"Then I kill them."

"Right. I feel we should definitely flesh this bit out. How are you going to make sure they don't all immediately scatter to the four winds when they realise they're under attack?"

It's a good point. The house and gardens are quite big and while I'm fast, so are vampires.

"Okay, so we have to make sure the fire funnels them towards me. Only light the back and sides of the building."

He nods slowly. "I'll toss some petrol bombs through the windows and you wait out the front."

It takes a lot of restraint not to knock him straight back. He reads the hesitancy in my eyes.

"Look, I have my stake gun. You can stop stressing."

"You have a stake gun?"

"Of course I do."

He goes over to his bag and digs deep into the bottom. What he pulls out looks more like a crossbow than a gun, but with its array of strings and hefty trigger, I can see its use.

"You've had that all the time?"

"Obviously, and silver-tipped wooden stakes to go with it."

"And you didn't think to mention that you had a small vampire-killing arsenal?"

He offers a nonchalant shrug and drops it back into the bag.

"You thought I was going to tackle them with my bare hands. Really? After the incident with Styx, I don't go to the bakers without that thing."

His self-deprecating laugh reminds me so much of the old Oliver, it almost makes me sad. He senses it too, and a moment passes between us. Like we are back in his apartment, arguing over who gets the last slice of pizza.

"Right then," his voice breaks the spell. "I saw some empty bottles in the basement and there's a petrol station on the way to the forest. We can use one of these God-awful floral sheets for the fuses."

"Okay," I say, agreeing to what is a significant improvement on my initial plan. "So that's it. We set fires on three sides of the house, leaving just the front for them to flee through. Then I take them out and you can get any strays with your gun, but at the same time making sure you stay well back. Is there anything else we need? Besides matches?"

"I don't think so."

"Then we're sorted."

Once again, we slip into silence and I run through everything one more time in my head, which takes all of five seconds. That's good though, isn't it? Aren't the best plans always the simplest? I hope so. I've not really been one for forward planning, as evidenced by all my previous life-and-death encounters. But normally, I'm on my own with no one to bounce ideas off. The fact that Oliver thinks this will work too, is reassuring. The annoying thing is that we have to wait until tomorrow. It feels a bit of an anticlimax.

"So, what should we do now?" I ask.

"I REALLY DON'T THINK THAT, NOW I'M A WEREWOLF, IT WAS a sensible idea to get drunk. In fact, it's actually pretty irresponsible of you."

"Me? Why am I the one to blame? I said we should have a drink. Sample some of the local ales. I didn't tell you to try all of them."

"But they were so good. And where are the ones we brought back with us? Did you put them in the fridge?"

I stand up with the intention of going to the kitchen, but my legs have other ideas, wobble and drop me straight back down on the sofa.

"We should stop now. You don't want to oversleep again tomorrow. We have to kill vampires, remember."

"Like I'd forget. It's fine. I'll give myself ten minutes

wolf time before I go to bed. I reckon that will prevent any hangover."

"You're going to change here? In the living room?"

"I can if I want to. Look." I stand up and start to unbutton my top.

"No!" Oliver grabs my wrists and pulls me down onto the sofa again, laughing. "No wolfing in the living room."

"Wolfing?"

"You heard me."

We dissolve into a fit of giggles. Again. Honestly, I can't remember the last time I laughed like this. Or laughed, full stop.

The plan had been to go out for dinner and enjoy our last evening here, making the most of the city we've seen so little of, before getting down to the small matter of killing vampires. And we did have fun. One drink led to another and then a few more. Over three hours later, we stumbled into the flat in hysterics.

"I've missed this," Oliver says, as if reading my thoughts.

"Missed it? I think this is only the third time I've seen you drunk in over five years."

"That's completely not true."

"Four then, perhaps."

"Well, I'm a responsible member of the community, don't you know?" he says in an over-exaggerated upper-class accent, tipping an invisible hat as he speaks. Then his eyes lock on mine with a seriousness we have managed to avoid all night.

"Can I ask you something?" he says.

"Sure, although only if you stop looking at me so weirdly. What is it?"

"Why him?"

The humour instantly evaporates with only the echo of laughter remaining.

"What do you mean?" I ask, as if I have no idea what he's talking about.

"You know what I mean. I don't want to be a dick about it, but when I think of you and him …" He stops, although the shudder says it all. "I just don't get it. You barely even knew him."

"I don't know what you want me to say."

Standing up, he takes a bottle from the fridge and knocks the cap off on the edge of the sink before taking a long pull.

"At the risk of sounding like a broken record, what has he got that I haven't? I'd do anything for you. Literally anything."

"I know that."

"I realise I've not had a century to work on my abs, but I'm not the worst-looking guy in the world. Am I?"

God, it really hurts to see someone like Oliver reduced to this. He's the type of bloke who girls find an excuse to give their phone numbers to, on the off chance he might call. To see him pining over me … is so wrong. Maybe completely drunk, the night before a raid on vampires, is the right moment to tell him, even if I do slur my words.

"Don't you get it? That's the whole point."

"I'm too good looking?"

"No, that you'd do anything for me."

He frowns, shaking his head. "And you don't want someone like that?"

"No, it's not that. I just feel like … I guess the thing is … I don't deserve you."

"What?"

He goes to take my hands, but I move them away. I can't let him hold me. The way I'm feeling, I know where it could lead.

"Naz, I've known from that first time I saw you …"

"It's a fantasy, Oliver. Yes, we have fun. You and Rey are, were, my best friends in the entire universe. But we—you and me—it couldn't work."

"Why not?"

"Because sooner or later, I'd let you down."

"Why do you say that? You wouldn't."

"Yes, I would. I would let you down, and I would break your heart."

"Well, I'm a big boy. I'll take the risk, and I just wish you would, too, rather than dismiss us so easily."

This is too much. My head is spinning and from more than just the drink. Of course, I know he has feelings for me. I'm not blind. Despite what I said, I want him, too. I think I always have. Just me and Oliver against the world. But it's not only about his heart, it's about mine, too. From the very first, I knew he was the type of guy who could break it. It's all so damn confusing. I take a deep breath and adopt a more serious tone.

"Honestly, it's just the drink talking. Besides, if you actually felt that way about me, why did you spend so many years with Rey?"

This question leaves him satisfyingly silent as he scratches an eyebrow.

"Rey was ... she and I were just messing around. You know that. Besides, it started before I even knew you."

"But you didn't stop it."

"Like I said, we were just messing around."

"Perhaps you preferred to be with someone you knew would never truly hurt you."

"That's not it."

"Then why? If you felt so strongly about me and you weren't worried I'd break your heart, then why didn't you do anything about it?"

"Because there was never a right time."

"And now is the right time?"

"No, now is definitely not the right time," he admits.

He looks defeated. Why do I do that? Why do I always push him away when what I really want is to have him closer? Maybe it couldn't be forever. Maybe not long at all. But right now, all I want to do is be with him.

"Why are you looking at me like that?" he asks, his eyes narrowing, suspiciously.

"Because I think I'm about to kiss you," I reply.

30

He sits motionless, not sure it's going to happen. Neither am I, until my mouth finally meets his. My eyes close, and a tingling sensation spreads out from my lips, flooding my whole body. I should definitely stop this now, but I feel like iron filings being drawn to a magnet.

After all these years, I thought it could only ever be friendship between us, something utterly platonic. It would be too weird for us to ever kiss, and there'd certainly never be a spark of anything if we did. Turns out I was entirely wrong. There are lots of sparks. It's like a static charge finally finding release, lighting up parts of me that have been in darkness my whole life. There's a warmth and tenderness I don't ever remember feeling. I move closer, desperate for more ... and he breaks away.

"You should get to bed," he says, grinning. "Tomorrow's a big day."

"But ... but ..."

"Tell you what: go to bed now, and I'll bring you breakfast in the morning. And I promise that the next time we kiss, you'll be a hundred percent sober."

"But why? Drunk kissing can be good, too. Drunk kissing can be very good, actually," I protest, then topple forwards.

"Night, Naz."

THE HEADACHE HITS ME FIRST. THEN THE MEMORY OF LIPS on lips and swarming butterflies in my stomach. Did that really happen? Shit, it did. I kissed Oliver! Or did he kiss me? No, the more I think about it, I kissed him. Wow. If I'd had to bet on him and me ever getting it on, I would have definitely put the money on him kissing me. Does it even matter which way round it was? Here we are. Shit.

Along with the confusion, there's the problem of what the hell I do now. How did we leave things? Oh God, this is just getting worse. We've had drunken nights together before without this happening, haven't we? Well, not many, clearly, but we have spent countless evenings slouched against one another on the settee, watching TV, and I've always managed to keep my lips separated from his. Well, they certainly didn't want to do that last night.

I pull the pillow over my head in mortification. How did I make such an idiot of myself? What else did I do? Did I tell him he was the last person I thought of when I thought I was going to die? No, surely not. I haven't even assimilated that myself yet. Shit! This is so much worse than just a mere physical hangover. At least I can take some paracetamol for that. But nothing's going to make this go away.

There's a rap on my door, followed by the creek of it opening.

"As promised," he says, switching the light on, then stepping in carrying a tray.

"Too bright!" I say, peeking out from under the pillow.

"Don't you remember? I said I'd make you breakfast in bed."

"You did?"

I lift the pillow fully and see the glint in his eye as he none-too-subtly runs his tongue around his lips. Shit, why am I even looking? What the hell is wrong with me? I pull the pillow back down over my head.

"Don't tell me my little wolf girl has a hangover. I thought you said a quick ten-minute change would sort that out."

My bed dips as he sits on it. God, please don't let him start talking about last night. I want to forget it ever happened. Or, rather, I want him to have forgotten.

"So, do you want to talk about last night?"

ARGH!!!!! Summoning all my strength, I throw the pillow at him.

"We have vampires to kill," I say, sitting up.

A smirk twitches on his lips. It's such an unbelievably cute smirk but I have the distinct urge to slap him.

"You're right," he says. "We do. So, I take it that means you don't want to talk right now."

"I don't know what you're on about."

He presses his lips together, managing to suppress whatever comment he was dying to make, then stands up and looks down at me.

"Eat breakfast. Kill vampires. Got it. But after that, you and I are going to have the conversation."

And he's gone.

How the hell do I get myself into these messes?

31

Thankfully, by the time I'm dressed and back in the living area, Oliver is in full-scale military mode and clearly has no time to think about such frivolous things as us kissing. For which I'm grateful.

"I brought those up from the basement," he says, passing me a cup of tea and gesturing to a crate of empty milk bottles. "I also found this." He indicates an old dark-green metal jerry-can. "We'll have to fill them when we get there. We can hardly walk through town with a box of Molotov cocktails."

"Okay, that's fine," I say, relieved that things are back to normal. I can take talk of homemade bombs over emotional stuff any day.

"And remember, when we're done, we need to move on as quickly as possible. We'll have to avoid public transport until we're well clear of the area, so it'll be back to hitching lifts. Anything you want to take, pack now. We won't be coming here again."

I hadn't considered that, and it makes me surprisingly sad. It took a bit of getting used to, but this place has been a home of sorts. I suppose part of me thought that once we'd killed the rogues, it'd be safe to stick around a bit longer, but of course, that's not the case. There's still the issue of the one that turned them in the first place. I nod.

"I'll get my bag."

Apart from two books I've yet to read, I leave the flat carrying little more than I arrived with over a month ago, all stuffed into a rucksack and strapped to my back.

We walk south, out of the town and towards the forest. We've followed this route every time we've gone training, but never in silence like this. Our minds are focused on what we're about to do. So much so, that I've almost forgotten what happened last night. Almost. Every now and then, I find my eyes drifting to him. Not staring exactly, just trying to read his thoughts. Annoyingly, every time I do this, he seems to catch me at it, and I end up quickly looking away and then blushing like some daft lovestruck teenage girl. This is ridiculous. He seems to think it's funny. So much for thinking it was going to be him finding it awkward.

Just outside the town, the petrol station comes into view. Oliver stops a hundred metres or so away and indicates for me to do the same.

"There'll be CCTV at the garage. We don't know how

this is going to pan out and we can't be seen buying the petrol. The last thing we want is the police on our tail.

"So how do we get it?"

Pursing his lips, he looks down the road and back again. He puts down the crate.

"Give me the can and wait here," he says.

He approaches a teenager walking our way. In less than ten minutes, we have our petrol, and the young lad has a twenty Euro note in his pocket.

It's just gone nine by the time we reach the forest. Normally, it would take me about twenty-minutes to get to the old house from here but that's running as a wolf, not walking as a human, weighed down with kit.

"Can you remember the way like this?" Oliver asks. "Or do you need to follow your nose, if that's appropriate wolf speak."

"I think I can do it like this," I reply, optimistically.

If I have to shift to wolf, that means becoming naked and he'd have to carry my shoes and clothes as well as my backpack and the petrol, not to mention his own things and the crate. Somewhat of a tall order. And to communicate or do anything requiring manual dexterity, I'd need to turn back and dress again. It's a pain in the butt and something they neglect to address in any of those werewolf films.

"Okay, given what you've told me about how far away the place is and how fast you run as a wolf, I estimate it'll take us about two hours walking. Does that sound about right?"

"I'm not great at all that speed-equals-distance-over-time stuff, but I think so."

"Well then, there's no need to rush. We should easily get there for around midday, which you say would be the best time to strike. Hopefully, the sky will stay clear."

I glance up. He's right. There's not a single cloud. If newly turned vampires come out in this, they won't stand a chance.

Thankfully, my time spent as a wolf seems to have improved my human sense of direction. There are one or two moments when I worry I may have got us lost—not that I let Oliver know this, obviously—but then I spot a familiar landmark and we're off again. That's the good news. The bad news is, it turns out to be much further away than I thought.

"I guess wolves run quicker than I realised," I say, as we stop for some water over an hour later, fully aware we haven't hit the halfway point yet. Part of me is tempted to run ahead and scout the place out, but then I'd have to wait for Oliver, so there'd be no point.

"You don't think you should know how fast you run?"

"Well, I don't have the benefit of a speedometer, and I assumed with your great wisdom, you'd be able to tell me if you thought I was wrong."

Given that I have no idea how fast I run as a human, I don't know why he'd imagine I'd be able to judge it as a wolf, but I stay quiet on the matter. We finish our drinks and continue on.

"You know, this feels like an army training exercise," I

tell him, switching the can to my right hand, the muscles down my left side having started to cramp.

"I bet you're glad now you did all those push-ups and pulls-ups, aren't you?"

"Not really. If I hadn't, I could have just feigned weakness and left you to carry everything."

"You know what, for someone so tenacious you can be exceptionally lazy."

"And proud to admit it."

He playfully bumps me.

"Hey! Be careful. I'll drop the fuel. And we should keep our voices down. We'll be in earshot soon."

After that, we walk in silence. Nerves begin to churn up my insides and unsettle my mind. Is this really a good idea, going after a nest of vampires? Sure, I've killed them before, but I had Calin by my side. Now I've got Oliver, and while he can hold his own against humans, we'll be dealing with something far more deadly.

Finally, we reach the break in the forest.

"That's it?" Oliver whispers.

"Yup."

"It's massive."

"Did I not mention that?"

"No, you didn't," he says, putting down the crate.

In my defence, I've always been a wolf when I've come here before, more often than not with my nose to the ground. But looking it now, it's more sizeable than I remember. How many bedrooms would a house like that have? Nine? Ten? A lot, that's for sure. Plenty of places for vampires to sleep. Maybe funnelling them out to the front won't be quite as easy as I hoped.

"Plan stands," Oliver says, obviously having had the same thought as me. "Let's get these bottles ready fast. You pour and I'll add the fuses."

"Okay," I say, and start to decant the petrol.

No going back now.

32

"I'll go around with you to the rear of the building," I say. "I want to make sure you're happy with the lie of the land but, more particularly, that nothing has changed since I was here last. It has been over twenty-four hours."

"All right. That makes sense."

Oliver politely turns away from me and I remove my clothes.

"Okay?" I ask the back of his head.

"As I'll ever be," he replies.

The wolf is ready for what's about to come. I close my eyes and feel my bones start to snap and morph. The pain is instantaneous, but it's an integral part of who I am now, and in a strange way, my body welcomes it.

Transition complete, I let out a low growl and he spins around. It's the first time he's been so close to me like this. He bends down and picks up my things, then stuffs them into a small bag that he slips onto his back. The rest of our possessions are stashed away in the bushes, so he only has the crate of Molotov cocktails to carry. His stake gun and stakes are strapped to his belt.

As we carefully skirt the building, my ears and nose are working overtime. I'm satisfied that everything seems the same. Reaching the back, I change again.

"Are you sure you want to do this?" I ask him.

"Yep. No going back now. It's time for you to get into position, while I light this place up,"

"Once it's burning, just stay back out of the way."

"Don't worry."

He pulls out a lighter from his pocket, then hesitates.

"What?" I ask.

"It's nothing."

"Oliver?"

"It's that, well, if anything does go wrong, I really wish our first kiss had been a sober one."

With all that's going on, this is still where his head is at?

"Well, if this goes right, our second kiss most definitely will be," I say.

"Naz, I just need you to know—"

His words cut out, as I transform into the wolf. They'll be plenty of time for flirting later.

I watch as he lights the first of the rags, then set off with a bound. I can now sense movement inside. The stench of death is overwhelming. But there's something else now, an undercurrent that I can't quite identify. I don't have time to dwell on it. I need to be ready for when they try to escape. As I reach the front of the house, I hear the smashing of glass and a whoosh as the petrol ignites. It's quickly followed by a second explosion and then more.

Please get out of the way as soon as you can, Oliver. God, let this work.

I can't see any fire yet, but the smell of smoke is strong, and I can hear panic within. Another window smashes followed by another whoosh. I pace back and forth, my eyes fixed on the front door.

Fire is now starting to spit and leap into the air above the roof. It makes it harder for me to focus on the sounds coming from inside. There's yelling. But how many voices are there? How many vampires?

The first one bolts out of the house, body bent over. He's pulled a T-shirt over his head, but his arms are still exposed, and the skin immediately starts to blister. He doesn't look where he's going, just blindly dashes for the cover of the forest, certainly not expecting to come across a werewolf. He barely has the chance to register a look of shock as I appear in front of him, then launch my teeth into his throat. They cut through his flesh like a hot knife through butter and when I pull back, I take a great chunk with me. As he staggers away, I leap on him and sever his head completely.

One down. How many more to go?

Two females burst out, screeching as they surge towards me, their exposed skin already starting to bubble. One of them collapses before she can even reach me, writhing in agony. I almost feel sorry for her. I've never thought much about what happens to vampire skin under the glare of sunlight. Now I know, and it's not a pretty sight.

The second is less exposed and is able to keep running. Her head goes from side to side as she looks for a way out. There isn't one. As she tries to dodge past me, I catch a flailing arm and swing her around like a ragdoll. There's a pop as her shoulder dislocates. I slam her to the ground and release her arm, but it's only a momentary reprieve. I grip her head in my powerful jaws, crush it like a melon and then rip it off. I turn back to the other one.

My muzzle is soaked in blood. For a moment, the face of the young vampire from the fight flickers into my mind. She was a killer, a monster, but had once quite likely been completely innocent, like these two probably were. But there's only black and white now, no shades of grey, no room for mercy. More vampires mean more humans taken to feed them, and I'm not going to let that happen on my watch.

The fire is spreading, and the house is well and truly ablaze. Stepping back, I stand poised, waiting for the next one to appear, wanting to dispatch it as swiftly as possible. I'm ready to pounce, only there's nothing to pounce on.

One minute passes, and then another. Still nothing. This feels wrong. I know I wasn't sure how many vampires there were, but I definitely sensed more than three. So where are they?

The penny drops with a sickening thud. They must have slipped out in another direction. Oliver's direction. As fast as I can, I race to the back of the house, thick black smoke swirling around me, catching in my throat.

Oliver! Oliver! I pray for him to hear me, but of course he can't.

As I reach the rear, a silhouette comes into view, well back from the blaze, almost at the line of trees. He's got himself out of harm's way, like he promised he would. I should remember I can always trust his word. I sprint towards him.

"Did they come this way?" I ask, shifting as I reach him, not caring about my nakedness anymore. "How many did you get?"

"None. I've not seen any. You?"

"Three."

"Only three?"

"I don't get it. I didn't sense any others leaving and I'm certain, positive, there were more than that."

"Well you are new to this whole sniffing-out-vampires thing. But it's good. It means there isn't some massive nest of rogues here. Why are you looking so concerned?"

"Something doesn't feel right."

Worry flickers in his eyes for a moment. He shakes his head and blinks it away.

"There's nowhere they could have gone. Look at the house. I did a pretty good job with the fire. Nothing could have survived that."

I see what he means. The remains of the roof have started to cave in, sending flaming tiles and chunks of wood crashing to the ground below.

"Here, get dressed." He throws me the bag and starts walking away. "We need to go."

I slip my dress over my head and prepare to follow, when a voice stops me dead in my tracks.

"Fancy seeing you two here."

33

I can't move. I'm dumbstruck. I've heard that voice a thousand times before, although recently only in my nightmares, screaming out my name. I could never have imagined that I would ever hear it again for real.

"Don't tell me you've forgotten your best friend already?" she says.

Tears immediately well up and I'm barely able to breathe. But I can't look back. I want to cling to this illusion for a little longer. But finally, I have to know.

As I turn towards the house, a gasp leaves my lips. It's Oliver who finds the words that I can't manage.

"Oh, my God! Rey! Rey, you're alive! You're alive!"

"Yes, I am," she replies.

Even seeing her in front of me and hearing her speak, I can't believe it's really true. Somehow, she's here. Somehow, she survived.

My knees start to buckle, but I manage to keep standing. It *is* her. It's Rey. Her flawless dark skin and perfectly curled hair, her sweet smile, are back in my life and suddenly everything else that's going on pales to insignificance. Rey is alive, and that's all that matters.

I turn to Oliver. With tears streaming down his cheeks, he races towards her, his breath jagged and his arms outstretched. Suddenly, barely a foot away, he jerks back as if he's slammed into a brick wall.

"I think that's close enough for now, don't you?" A second voice causes me to spin back around.

I hate to say that I fit people into stereotypes, based on their looks, but this woman falls into one so perfectly, she's practically a caricature. She must be close to seventy, with jet black hair reaching down to her waist, but with white roots. She's dressed in black jeans, black top and black boots, with dozens of silver bangles. It's safe to say she's a witch.

Midway between me and Rey, Oliver is rooted to the spot.

"Rey?" he whispers, still not moving. Her hand is held towards us, palm out and something sparks in her eyes. It must be a blocking spell. Magic. Real magic.

"How?" It's the only word I can manage. She answers with the slightest of laughs.

"How did I get my powers? Or how did I survive being left to die in a feeding frenzy of vampires?"

There's a snideness to her comment, so unlike the old Rey that it causes my skin to prickle.

"Enough of this," the other witch says. "You know the orders."

"Who the hell are you?" I demand.

"Oh, I'm so sorry, we haven't been formally introduced, have we? My name is Tamsin. Actually, we were both recently holidaying in Scotland, at the same time."

A sly smile twists on her lips.

"Funnily enough, I met some werewolves there, too. At least they said they were, but they seemed to be having trouble shifting.

"You!" I gasp, a fresh wave of nausea hitting me. "You made the potion. You stopped them from changing. You were working with the vampires."

"I don't know what you're talking about." She smiles. Her mouth is full of blackened teeth and her eyes are unnaturally dark against her pale skin. "I have been known to create tonics, for a certain fee. I'm afraid I can't divulge my customers' identities, though. Client privilege, you understand."

Alena was the name of the wolf who was brought back to my mother's camp the night Calin and I arrived. Her body was so battered, she was barely recognisable. But what worried the pack most, was why she hadn't changed to a wolf, either to escape her attackers or to help herself heal. Calin had guessed that night that a witch could be working in cahoots with a vampire. And now here she is, standing in front of me.

The wolf howls inside, but it's the human me that

lunges for her. I've barely moved a foot before my body is snared by invisible shackles and I'm stuck fast.

"I'm going to kill you," I hiss, with all the venom I possess.

Her smile widens. "I'm afraid that's not part of the plan. You will be coming with us. And your friend here. I'm afraid he's already seen too much."

Oliver sets his face with grim determination and reaches for his gun. But before he can clear it from the holster, invisible restraints have his hands pinned in the air. The blood drains from his face as, step by step, the witch approaches. I may be against old people being abused, but I feel I can allow myself to make an exception in this case.

The wolf growl intensifies inside me. I'm a split second away from unleashing it, when Rey speaks again.

"Actually," she says, "there's a new plan."

"Andrea?" The older witch looks unsure.

"I think you've taken me as far as you can, Tamsin," Rey says, lifting her chin slightly. "I do appreciate everything you've taught me, though. I really do."

"Don't do this. Andrea, don't—"

Her final words hang in the air, drifting off into the ether, as with a flick of Rey's wrist, she drops to ground.

34

For a second, I think it's faked—some kind of immersive drama experience—but it's not. The old woman lies still, an expression of disbelief frozen on her face.

She killed her. Rey has killed her. And she saved Oliver.

"Oh God, Rey."

I go to hug her. I want to squeeze her tighter than anyone has ever been squeezed in their entire life and never let her go. But the invisible binding that stopped me is now tightening around my chest. It's becoming hard to breathe.

"You ... You escaped, Rey. Thank God you escaped. Thank God." Tears roll down my cheeks.

"Come now, Narissa," she says, walking towards me. "I didn't expect this reunion to be quite so emotional. There again, I expect you thought you'd seen the last of me, when you left me."

"I'm so sorry. So sorry," I gasp.

I'm on the ground now. I look up at Oliver. He too is struggling to breathe.

"Sorry for what, Narissa?" She crouches down to my level and locks her eyes on mine. "Leaving me there, or not even bothering to come and look for me later?"

Reaching out her hand, she brushes away a tear. The touch of her skin against mine feels like an electric shock. Her eyes flash, black and venomous, unlike anything I've ever seen in her before.

"What has happened to you?" I ask.

I try again to move, but invisible forces still hold me. She stands up, throws back her head and laughs. The bindings suddenly disappear and we're set free. Oliver topples over, coughing, and I rush to his side.

"Quick, Narissa, help him. There she is, Oliver." Contempt oozes from her lips. "You know what? I waited for you. For both of you. I was so sure *you* would come for me," she says, looking at Oliver. "The way *I* would have come for you. Guess I'm not as important to you as your precious little Narissa. Days turned into weeks. And nothing. Nothing at all."

"We thought you were dead, Rey." Oliver approaches her, but she throws him back with another flick of her hand. He lands on his back, yelling in pain. I recoil, holding back a scream.

"Rey, please—"

"Please. Please. Please. Does that remind you of anything, Narissa? I begged you, Narissa. I *begged* you to help me."

"There was no way I could. There were too many vampires. You disappeared."

"And what about in the dungeon? What about then?"

"The dungeon?" I'm confused. "How do you know about that?"

"I could sense you there, Narissa. It *was* you; I know it was. I heard you sobbing, and I called out to try and comfort you. But you didn't give me a second thought when it came to getting yourself out of there, did you? I begged you to save me, too. But you just didn't care, did you?"

"I thought ... I thought ..." Tears once again stream down my face. I remember thinking I heard her voice, almost feeling her presence there. But I was so sure it was all part of my constant nightmares, one of the voices in my head that haunted me night and day.

"Rey, if I had believed for one minute that you were still alive, I would have moved heaven and earth to get to you. I would have killed every vampire in London."

"Even the one that you've been screwing? I will admit, it was Tamsin who had the sight. She was pretty useless at magic, but she did have some skill there. Keeping track of you. Visions and the like. But I'll manage without her. And don't worry, we've not told anyone about you and the vampire *yet*. I wanted to have my fun with you first, but I'll let him know when I return. Make sure that special friend of yours suffers."

"*Him?*" Who is she talking about?

"Polidori of course," she says, as if it's quite obvious.

"The vampires," Oliver says, joining the dots. "They

gave you access to the grimoires, in exchange for you finding Naz."

"That, amongst other things. You know, they really can be rather agreeable once you get to know them."

"What have you done, Rey?" Oliver's voice is barely a whisper.

Spinning around, she spits her words at him.

"What have *I* done? What have *I* done? I've taken care of *myself*. That's what I've done. All those empty words and broken promises. You. Narissa. Blackwatch. Even my own family abandoned me. Well, I don't need any of you now. I've got all the power I'll ever need. And when the uprising comes, I will be on the winning side. Not that you'll be around to see it."

The uprising. That's what the young rogue girl was talking about. She wanted to know if I was going to be part of it.

"Rey, whatever this is, we can work together. You can't trust vampires."

She laughs that same laugh again. So callous and cold. So different from the Rey I knew. My Rey. The real one.

"I won't ever trust anyone anymore. Don't you see? That was my big mistake all along. Well, that's done and dusted." She stops and frowns. "That reminds me. Aren't you here for a reason? Isn't there something you should be doing? I admire your plan—simple but effective—using the midday sun to your advantage. I'd be interested to see how well you fare without it."

Lifting her arms to the sky, she starts speaking in a

CHAPTER 34

foreign tongue that I don't recognise. Rounded vowels. Sharp constants. I have no idea what it means, but I'm guessing from the way every hair on my body is now standing on end that it's not good. What happens next confirms this. It's like a scene from some crazy end-of-days movie. I look up. The clear blue that was there only moments ago, is turning a deep purple as clouds form. In a minute, they go from thin and wispy to thick and threatening and totally blot out the sun. Then they start to swirl above us. Literally swirl.

"You know, when I first practised magic, I couldn't do anything at a distance, other than that trick with glass, of course. I had to start with the basics, hands on. There were the potions, too. You know, like the one that helped you heal faster after Joe beat you up. Or the one Tamsin made to stop those wolves turning. But she never truly embraced the power. Never allowed it to fill her, as I have done. It's so much easier now that I'm totally free of all constraints. But I'm not complacent. There are still things I need to learn. But one or two new good spells at a time suits me fine."

Interspersed with talking to us, she continues with the other language. She sounds like a rambling crazy woman.

Suddenly, Oliver is beside me, looking really scared.

"Naz, the house ..."

I immediately see where his fear's coming from. Of course, Rey already knows what's caught his attention.

"Controlling the elements is something I'm quite good at."

I can't focus on what she's saying anymore. The cloud

cover in place, well over a dozen vampires are emerging unscathed from the fire-ruined building. A protective sphere surrounds each of them. Shit.

Could I deal with them like that? I'll give it a damn good try. But now it's not only Oliver I've got to worry about; there's Rey too. Whatever's going on, the real Rey's got to be in there somewhere, still. We must get her to safety.

"It was easy enough to protect them from the flames and keep them penned in. Like I said, a couple of new spells at a time. But I guess the change in the weather has encouraged them to come out to play. Oopsie!"

She sneers, her eyes narrowing in the most vicious of smiles I've ever seen.

"Now, Narissa. I believe you're quite a fighter. Let's hope it's true. For both your sakes."

35

Twenty vampires are not that many. Really, they're not. They are already nervous, likely having seen what happened to their friends. I've just got to keep them away from Oliver and Psycho Rey. The wolf is ready. I think it's looking forward to the challenge. I can feel it growling in my head. I already disposed of three easily enough. I can do this.

"I've got this," I say to Oliver as I strip off my dress and prepare to transform.

Nothing happens.

I try again. Try? I haven't ever had to do that. It's pure instinct. Second nature. The moment I will it, it happens. Yet here I am, still one-hundred-percent human, as a horde of vampires, who can see I'm panicking, tentatively move towards us.

"Any second now would be great, Naz."

Oliver has a stake in one hand and a loaded gun in the

other, ready to fire but holding off doing so. I understand why. Right now, they're moving towards us slowly, confused and cautious. They're all new, just like the girl at the fight was, and bemused by this sudden blanketing of the sky. The minute he shoots, all hell is going to break loose, and I really need to be the wolf when that happens.

"Oh dear. What's wrong?" Rey asks with mock sincerity. "Are you suffering from performance anxiety? What a terrible time for it to happen. I was so looking forward to seeing you up close as this wolf I've heard so much about. But I'm sure you'll be okay. From what I've seen, your kind are pretty tough even in human form, aren't they?"

I suddenly realise what's going on.

"This is you. You're stopping me from changing, aren't you?"

Her sneer widens.

"Can you blame me for wanting a little entertainment? After all, you were more than happy to leave me to suffer."

"I thought you needed a potion to do this?" I'm shaking and I feel sick.

"Tamsin needed a potion. Did I not already mention how much stronger than her I am?"

"Rey, please. You've made your point."

"Naz, we need to focus here," Oliver says and tosses me a spare stake. "Remember your training and go for the heart."

"So I have to fight them with a stick, butt naked. Brilliant."

"They're fast and strong, but it's unlikely they're skilled

CHAPTER 35

fighters," he says. "Go for those that are closest first. Start with that one on the far right."

My eyes follow where he indicates. There's still a fair distance between us and the vampires, but if they start running, they'll be on us in a second. Many of them are still confused, staring up at the sunless sky, but others have clocked us and are snarling, fangs exposed.

Oliver takes a shot and one of them goes down, clutching its chest.

It's safe to say they have all noticed us now.

I move towards the one closest to me and plunge the stake into him but miss his heart. I yank it back out but not quickly enough to avoid him striking me. The blow hurts, a throbbing pain shooting up from my shoulder, but it's not enough to slow me down. Instead, I use the momentum as I fall and roll forwards to spring up behind him. The stake goes in clean this time, but I can't stop to congratulate myself. Before I've had a chance to figure out which one to go for next, another is in front of me. They're starting to get more organised, making use of their speed to surround us.

Oliver takes down a second with his gun but doesn't have time to do more than snatch another stake from his belt before two more snarling vamps descend on him. He may know what he's doing, but his encounter with Styx and the beating at the fight club mean he's not at full strength, and without the gun loaded, he's stuck with just a stake in his hand. It's pretty obvious he needs help.

"Hold on!" I yell to him. "I'm coming to you."

Getting there is easier said than done, as I'm currently surrounded myself. I kick out at the knees of the nearest rogue, taking her by surprise and dashing through the gap that opens up. I loop my arm around the neck of one of his attackers and hurl it backwards. I'm sure I hear its neck snap, but I have no idea how long that will keep it down. Oliver uses my sudden arrival as the distraction he needs to stake the other one. Five down. Only another fifteen to go. But it looks like we're now penned in.

"Watch out on your right!" he yells.

I catch the vampire clean across the face with a high kick. It stumbles but responds with a retaliatory punch. I duck and bring my stake up cleanly under its ribcage. I turn back to Oliver. One is on him. He's fighting but not like he ever did with me in training—this is real fighting. Fighting for survival. One punch, then another, lands hard on the vampire, but it's so strong it barely even flinches. Why hasn't he staked it? Then I see the problem; his stake is wedged in its back.

"Oliver, catch!" My shout attracts not only his attention but also that of the vampire he's engaged with. Which is good on two counts. By the time it realises what is about to happen, I've thrown Oliver my stake. He snatches it out of the air and plunges it into the vampire's chest then withdraws it with a twist of his wrist.

"Just hold on to this one, will you?" I say, managing a brief smile.

He quickly loads the gun again and we go back-to-back, turning in circles to keep the wary vamps at bay, as Oliver passes me a replacement stake from his belt.

"Look at you two, working together. You know it's such a shame. I've always thought you'd make a lovely couple. Of course, you'd need to be alive for that to happen."

Rey's voice is beginning to really grate on me.

"When this is over," I mutter, "I swear I'm going to get her back."

I wave my weapon at a vampire that's inched to within just three feet of me.

"I've never tasted fresh blood before," he hisses, flashing his fangs at me. Then his hand flies up and catches my stake.

My mouth goes dry and my heart is racing as I rip it back from his grasp.

"Sorry to disappoint you, but that isn't going to happen today, either," I tell him.

I dart out a hand, grab him around the neck and jerk him forwards onto the other one, which is holding the stake.

Oliver continues to hold the rest at bay, waving his gun at them.

"How many stakes have you got left?" I whisper.

"Not enough."

If I could just change ... I look towards Rey, who is enjoying the spectacle.

"Shoot her!" I mutter.

"What!"

"Shoot her! We have to break her concentration."

Without further ado, he changes aim and fires.

The tiny silver-laced missile catches her in the shoulder. It takes her a split second to realise what's happened. She lets out a scream and clutches at the injury. As she does so, the clouds part, and a shaft of sunlight beams down onto the remaining vampires below. They start screaming, too, and fall to their knees in agony.

Oliver seizes the opportunity, quickly reloads and begins taking down more vampires. But my attention is on Rey, who is doubled over. Now is my chance. I start to shift. I feel the bones crack and move, but they aren't resetting! What should be a moment of fleeting agony prolongs into seconds. Through my tears, I see the horror on Oliver's face.

Rey looks up, her whole body trembling as her eyes darken into bottomless pits. I focus with everything I've got on completing the change. I feel the bones setting at last— but they've gone back into human configuration!

"You tried to kill me!" she shrieks, full of hate and fury.

"Rey, we're trying to save you," I shout above the cries of the vampires.

"I am saved! You will pay for this."

As she lifts her hands to the sky once more, Oliver points the gun at her again.

"Rey, don't make me do it," he says, his face set hard.

"Oliver, no!" I scream, but he's not listening. He knows this is the only way. In my heart of hearts, I do too. But this is Rey.

She opens her mouth as his finger tenses on the trigger.

Time slows down. He'll hit her, without any doubt. And this time, he's aiming to kill. As his finger flexes, I throw myself at him, sending the projectile just millimetres wide of her head.

"You will suffer, like I suffered!" she screeches at us.

Her arms lifting into the air are the last things I see before we're suddenly plunged into total darkness. The type that terrifies children and adults alike. We're fighting blind.

"Oliver!"

"Keep going, Naz!" he yells back. "I love you. And Rey, I'm so sorry! I love you both so much."

"Don't you dare give up," I yell back.

This can't be it. There has to be a way out. I've thought I was going to die too many times recently for it to actually happen now. Not like this. I scream at the wolf, but it's trapped. Shackled inside me.

"Rey!" I shout with all the force I can muster. "This is on me. Let him go! He's your best friend. Please, Rey! You've got me. They can have me. Just let Oliver go! Please!"

"How, sweet. You really do care for him, don't you, Narissa? Trust me, I'm doing you guys a favour. It'll all be over soon."

She's right. I feel their breath, smell the stench of death on them. I lash out time and again, but all I'm connecting with is air. Nothing else. I'm done. I'm nearly choking on my tears. This is it. This is how I die. And the vampires are just the tool. I was the one who set the ball rolling and I'm to be murdered by someone I once loved but let down in the worst possible way. I suppose she thinks it's fair. An eye for an eye.

Something cold grabs my arm. Screaming, I strike out wildly and connect with the vampire's face. Its grip loosens, but only for a second.

"I love you, Rey!" I call into the abyss. "I'm sorry. I'm sorry I couldn't save you."

A shriek rings out.

"Oliver!" My heart is breaking.

"I'm here, Naz! I'm still here!"

There's a rush of air in front me and the vampire who'd just grabbed my arm is gone. Silence follows.

"What's happening?" I ask.

Stumbling backwards, I tread on something warm and fleshy and jump away in horror.

"Oliver?"

"Naz?"

"What's going on?"

Above us, the clouds are swirling again, and light is starting to break through. A voice cuts through the gloom. One that doesn't belong here. It's young, full of optimism and hope. And it's speaking in a series of short, rushed sentences.

"Hope you don't mind. Kind of thought you were having a rough time. We're all having a rough time at the minute though, aren't we? Anyway, we just thought we'd give you a hand, even the odds up a bit."

36

The clouds race away now, as if driven by a great wind, sent back to wherever they came from, leaving just clear blue sky. Then things move so fast, I'm not sure what happens first.

I turn to Rey. She's on the ground. Unconscious, but still breathing, a large wolf standing over her.

The wolf in me is free at last and I transform.

It appears she wasn't able to stop so many of us all shifting at once.

Lou, is it really you?

I look around. The vampires are all dead and there are over a dozen wolves standing in their place.

Narissa.

The voice that now comes through to me warms my heart almost as much as Lou's did.

Chrissie! How did you find us? How did you know? Who else is here?

We have people on the inside and one of them came here to investigate. He heard you when he was out scouting. He also smelled the vampire nest.

How did you get here so quickly?

I sense her smiling inside her head. It's a feeling I thought I would never experience again. I missed being part of the pack, but until this moment, I hadn't realised quite how much. Her voice comes through again.

Well, it helps when you have rich friends.

She tilts her head towards the forest. It's hard to make out anything. The sky is once again clear, but the canopy is so dense everything beneath it is in deep shadow.

But then I see him, standing at the edge. Calin. He came for me.

I race towards him, as a wolf, but I don't care. I've nearly reached him, when something stops me dead in my tracks. Why am I running to him? He's not the one who needs me. Changing into human form, I offer him little more than a nod before turning and dashing back the other way.

He's lying on the grass. Two of the pack are bending over him, human now. For a moment, I think the worst.

"Oliver!"

"I'm fine," he says, waving a hand in the air, although I'm not sure if that's directed at me or the two naked men. "I'm fine."

He pushes himself up to sitting position. Straight away, I notice there are bite marks on his arms and possibly others I can't see. They're deep by the looks of things, and blood is still pouring liberally from the wounds. Wounds each comprising four puncture marks. From top *and* bottom fangs.

"That doesn't look fine at all," I say.

"Trust me, it could have been a lot worse. Surprisingly, it doesn't hurt that much."

"We need to get you help."

"I'm sure the bleeding will stop soon. It's not as bad as it looks."

"I thought I'd lost you."

"Yeah, I don't mind admitting it was touch and go there for a moment."

The others have moved away to give us some privacy. A fully dressed pack member seems to be handing out clothes. I scan the ground in vain for my dress. When I turn back, Oliver is holding it out in front of him and I slip it over my head. I feel the tears building in my eyes.

"I so sorry for everything." I place my hand against his cheek. His warmth is reassuring. "I'm sorry for getting you into this. For Rey. Oh God, Rey."

I twist around. She's out cold, and with four wolves guarding her, she's unlikely to be going anywhere until they decide otherwise.

"She'll be okay." He takes my hand. "*We'll* be okay. We'll find a way to fix this," he says, with such conviction I can almost believe him. "And just so you know, I'm definitely going to hold you to that kiss."

I think he means now, and I lean in towards him, but he puts a hand up to stop me.

"I think there's someone you need to thank first, for both of us," he says.

I look over towards Calin before turning back to Oliver. "You're sure it's okay?"

"Depends on what you're asking, but yes, I'm fine for you to go thank the bloodsucker. I'll check on Rey."

I don't run straight to Calin. Instead, I help Oliver up, trying not to show my concern at his injuries. When he's steady on his feet, I walk towards the forest.

The shadows of the leaves are creating a dappled pattern on his skin. I'm not sure if I want to kiss him or hit him, so decide to do neither.

"Swooping in to rescue me again, I see."

"Technically, the wolves are the ones who did the rescuing. I just helped them with the swooping-in part."

"Private helicopter?"

"Chartered plane. A helicopter wouldn't fit all these guys in. You should know that."

He's trying to make light of things, but right now, I'm struggling to see the humour in any of it. He sent me away —without him.

"You could have spoken to me. You could have let me know you were okay."

"I should have done."

"Too right you should have." I gesture back towards Rey. "Polidori sent her. And she knows about us, which means he must, too. You can't go back to the Council."

He nods and stares at me, saying nothing, so I keep talking. "This vampire nest, I believe there may be more of them. I think there's something big planned. An uprising, one of them said."

"We'll find out what it is."

Maybe it's the lack of privacy, with Oliver and all the others nearby. It's probably hard for him to say what he would like to, but there's some sort of weird reticence going on here, as if he isn't telling me everything. Whatever it is, the state of our relationship comes way down the list. First, I need to deal with Rey and work out what's going on with her and Polidori.

"We'll have to work together on this," I say, "And we'll need Freya to rally the wolves. Where is she by the way? Did she stay in Scotland with the rest of the pack?"

In barely the time it takes a normal person to blink, he lowers his eyes to the ground and back up again. But I see it, and I know exactly what it means. And the world falls away beneath my feet.

EPILOGUE

I'm officially an orphan, again. Isn't that often the way it is for the heroes of films or books? Only this isn't that. This is my real life. You'd think I would have already grieved enough for her the first time around. I've spent most of my life pining for the mother I lost, who I barely knew. But this time, I feel I did know her, and that makes the pain seem even worse.

We drive out of the town in convoy: the remaining wolves of the north pack, Calin, Oliver and I.

And Rey.

I don't know where we're heading. Calin only says we're going somewhere safe, that's suitable to take us all, and that's enough for me right now.

Lou is asleep on the back seat next to me.

She filled me in on what happened: Juliette's brutal arrival, the scattering of the wolves, the spies they have inside South Pack who feed them information when they can. One of those was the wolf I sensed the other day. Thank God it was him who Juliette sent to look for me. Anyone else, and I'd probably be dead.

Staying alive is our main aim at this moment in time. That and sorting out Rey. Calin bound her hand and foot then gagged her, before knocking her out with a huge dose of vampire venom. It's safe to say he's not going to take any chances with her. And neither will I.

Werewolves and vampires be damned, I'm on a mission now: to get my best friend back.

WANT TO FIND OUT IF REY CAN BE REDEEMED? AND IS Calin's promised safe haven really as safe as he thinks? All will be revealed in Dark Redemption, Book 4 of the Dark Creatures Saga, so get it now!

SCAN ME

Want to witness Rey's discover of her magical abilities? Claim your collection of FOUR prequel novellas to enjoy her very own origin story? PLUS, get information on new releases and exclusive content.

NOTE FROM ELLA

First off, thank you for taking the time to read **Dark Deception**, Book 3 in the Dark Creatures Saga. If you enjoyed the book, I'd love for you to let your friends know so they can also experience this action-packed adventure. I have enabled the lending feature where possible, so it is easy to share with a friend.

If you leave a review **Dark Deception** on Amazon, Goodreads, Bookbub, or even your own blog or social media, I would love to read it. You can email me the link at ella@ellastoneauthor.com

Don't forget, you can stay up-to-date on upcoming releases and sales by joining my newsletter, following my social media pages or visiting my website
www.ellastoneauthor.com

ACKNOWLEDGMENTS

First off thank you to Christian for his amazing covers for the whole series and Carol for her diligent editing.

To Lucy, Kath and all the alpha and beta readers who have helped shape this novel, I'd be lost without you.

And lastly, thank you to all of you readers out there for taking a chance on my book. I hope it has bought you as much joy reading it as it did for me writing it.

Printed in Great Britain
by Amazon